KLUTZHOOD

KLUTZHOOD

CHRIS McMAHEN.

ORCA BOOK PUBLISHERS

Library and Archives Canada Cataloguing in Publication

McMahen, Chris
Klutzhood / written by Chris McMahen.

ISBN 978-1-55143-710-1

I. Title.

PS8575.M24K58 2007   jC813'.54   C2007-902768-7

First published in the United States, 2007

Library of Congress Control Number: 2007927449

Summary: Arlo is the new kid in town—and he's not about to blend in just to make his mother happy.

Orca Book Publishers gratefully acknowledges the support for its publishing programs provided by the following agencies: the Government of Canada through the Book Publishing Industry Development Program and the Canada Council for the Arts, and the Province of British Columbia through the BC Arts Council and the Book Publishing Tax Credit.

Cover and text design by Teresa Bubela
Cover artwork by Monika Melnychuk
Author photo by Ben McMahen

ORCA BOOK PUBLISHERS
PO Box 5626, STN. B
VICTORIA, BC CANADA
V8R 6S4

ORCA BOOK PUBLISHERS
PO Box 468
CUSTER, WA USA
98240-0468

www.orcabook.com
Printed and bound in Canada.
Printed on 100% PCW paper.
10 09 08 07 • 4 3 2 1

To the staff, students and parents at Highland Park Elementary School in Armstrong, British Columbia, and to the Golden Agers Hockey Sanatorium for their inspiration and perspiration.

ACKNOWLEDGMENTS

I was once told that a writer trying to get a manuscript published is like a centipede attempting to cross a six-lane freeway. I'd like to thank my wife, Heather, for diverting traffic, helping me tie up all those pairs of laces, and standing on the far side of the road waving encouragement. Thanks also to Emily and Ben for watching out for centipedes as they cruise down life's highway. I'd also like to thank fellow centipedes Margriet Ruurs, John Lent and the Long Lake Writers for their expertise and unwavering enthusiasm. Finally, my thanks to Sarah Harvey, editor extraordinaire, for giving this centipede flying lessons.

CHAPTER 1

I hadn't had so much fun since the time I got locked out of the house in my underwear. Today was my first day at a brand-new school in a brand-new town. I arrived at the drop-off area in front of the school in a rusty old pickup truck with *Fast Eddy's Manure Sales* written across both doors and a load of guess-what in the back. A crowd of people lined the sidewalk, staring at the heap of a pickup: one headlight missing, the front bumper held on with twisted wire, and an engine that backfired so often it sounded like a fireworks display on wheels.

The driver of the truck—my mom—didn't help make my arrival exactly smooth. She wasn't used to the gear-shift, so every time she tried to shift gears it sounded like an out-of-whack dentist's drill, and the truck would lurch forward, hopping like a gigantic, manure-filled, metal Easter bunny. When we finally pulled up to the curb, the engine let off a final ear-splitting *BANG*! before it died.

With all those strangers staring at me from the sidewalk, I refused to get out of the truck. No one—not even my mom—could make me get out and walk through that crowd and go inside to register at my new school.

I have had many embarrassing moments in my life. I mentioned the underwear incident. And then there was the time I accidentally ate cat food at a friend's birthday party. But neither of those times came close to the embarrassment I felt with all those people staring at me like I was an alien in a manure-powered UFO.

You might be wondering what brought me to this horrible situation. To fully understand why I was going to a new school in the first place, and why I arrived in a manure truck in the second place, I have to take you back a couple of weeks to when my life wasn't quite so awful.

"East Bend? East Bend? Where in the world is East Bend?" I screamed. "Why can't we move to somewhere I've heard of, like New York or Moscow or Tuktoyaktuk! But East Bend? It's probably so small it's not even on the road map! But it doesn't matter because no one ever goes there anyway!"

"It's a couple of hundred kilometers west of the Alberta border," Mom continued, trying to remain calm as she delivered news she knew I wouldn't want to hear. But I could tell by the tiny quiver in her voice that she wasn't exactly as cool as a cucumber.

After my dad died two years ago, Mom went back to school to upgrade her nursing degree. She talked about how much better things would be for us when she landed her first job. We wouldn't have to shop at secondhand stores all the time, I could go to the movies with my friends more often, and we'd have way more money to buy all the stuff we'd been doing without.

One day I came home from school and found balloons and streamers hanging from the ceiling and a double-deluxe pizza sitting on the table. Mom was dancing around the apartment like she had red-hot coals in her socks. I hadn't seen Mom act like this since before Dad got sick.

"Whose birthday?" I asked.

"It's no one's birthday, silly!" she giggled. "We are celebrating the beginning of our new life, Mr. Arlo P. Billingsly! I found out today that I've been hired for a nursing job! Isn't that great?"

Of course I was thrilled. This would mean pizza more often, moving to a better apartment, cable TV, a new computer and clothes that weren't hand-me-downs from my cousin, Bruno! Life would be a lot easier for Mom and me—and a whole lot more fun. I couldn't wait to tell Zack and Bo that it was only a matter of time before Mom could afford to buy me that new BMX bike I had my eye on. After inhaling the pizza and guzzling down some root beer, I'd charge down to the park to give my best buddies the great news.

It was good to see Mom cheerful again. Going to school, working part-time as a housecleaner and trying to take care of me, all at the same time, had made her fuse a lot shorter than when Dad was alive.

"Of course," she added, looking me right in the eye, "my new job will mean some changes."

Sure there would be changes. I knew this. But the changes were all good. But the way Mom was looking at me, I suddenly wasn't so sure. She wasn't smiling anymore.

"My new job isn't in Victoria, Arlo. It's in a small town called East Bend. We'll be moving there at the beginning of next month."

To say I was in shock would not really describe how I reacted to Mom's news.

That's when I started yelling, "East Bend? East Bend? Where in the world is East Bend?" After she explained where this dumpy little town was located, I paused and stared at her, waiting for her face to crack into a smile, and for her to yell, "April Fool!" even though it wasn't April. I waited, but Mom's face didn't change.

"You're kidding, Mom, aren't you? Please tell me you're not serious!" I pleaded.

"I know how attached you are to your friends, Arlo, but I couldn't find a full-time public health job in Victoria. The job offer from East Bend was the best I got. No shift work. Great benefits."

"East Bend? East Bend? What kind of a name is that! Why couldn't we move to a place called Surf City or

Junkfoodville!?" I was screaming again. I always scream when I'm upset.

"There's no need to panic, Arlo. It sounds like a lovely little town. A friend of mine used to live there. She says you'll love it." Mom had a pleading look in her eyes, as if she really expected me to be as excited about moving to Nowheresville as she was. "A lot of the kids play ice hockey there, so it'll be a new experience for you."

"If people were meant to play ice hockey, they wouldn't have teeth!" I yelled. "Plus, I think I'm allergic to small rubber disks! And besides, my feet think skates are foreign objects!"

"You're overreacting, Arlo." I could tell by the tone of her voice that she was losing patience with me. Moving to East Bend was a done deal, no matter what I thought.

"Overreacting? Overreacting!" I screamed. "I'm not overreacting! Do you realize, Mother, that I am probably the only kid my age in Canada who can't skate? The only ice I've ever seen floats in a glass!"

Victoria doesn't have cold winters like most other places in Canada. We were lucky to get a few days of snow each year. Some kids played ice hockey on indoor rinks, but my friends and I didn't. Instead we played soccer, rode our bikes and raced in a swim club. Once in a while we might play road hockey, but the closest I ever came to skating was when I watched *Hockey Night in Canada*. And I didn't even do that very often.

"And just how 'little' is this little town?" I said, not quite screaming this time. "Like, the entire population will be you, me and some old guy who lives in a cave and wears animal skins?"

"Arlo, calm down. I know you're upset but…"

You bet I was upset. I'd lived in Victoria all my life. I was born in Victoria! I got toilet trained in Victoria! My dad taught me how to ride a bike in Victoria! I did my first six and a half years of school in Victoria! All my friends were there, my swim team was there, and that's where I belonged. It was home! Home wasn't some dumpy little town called East Bend. Maybe my mom wanted to start over with a new career in a new town, but not me. I was happy just where I was. It was her idea to move. Not mine. I wasn't going to make it easy for her.

After my first few attempts at changing her mind didn't work, I got desperate. I pleaded. I begged. I even tried bribing her with my life savings, which I kept in a smelly sock under the bed. But she wouldn't change her mind—not even for $8.70 worth of nickels, dimes and quarters. Two weeks later, we were driving through the mountains to East Bend.

It was February. That meant snowy highways. My mom wasn't used to driving in snow, so she drove at a speed that was only slightly faster than a lame turtle.

"Driving in snow is part of our new experience, Arlo," she said, gripping the steering wheel so hard her knuckles turned pure white. "It's one of the many new challenges facing us." Along with white knuckles, Mom's eyes widened to about twice their normal size as we crept along the Coquihalla Highway through a blizzard, with only a pair of tire tracks to guide us.

It took us two whole days to drive to East Bend. That gave me forty-eight hours to try to convince Mom to turn around and forget this lousy moving idea.

"I bet they only get one TV channel in East Bend," I whined. "And it probably only shows *Gilligan's Island* reruns all day and all night long!"

"Arlo, I'm sure there's more than one TV channel. They probably have..."

"And there's probably no McDonald's! Just some dirty, greasy, fast-food place run by gangsters who drop cigarette butts in the hamburgers and make milkshakes out of whipped asparagus!"

"Arlo, I'm sure there's a good place to eat..."

"And I bet they get snow eleven and a half months of the year! And for the other two weeks the mosquitoes are so big you have to swat them with aluminum baseball bats!"

"Arlo, the climate's not that..."

"And I bet they used to have a swim team, but everyone died when they were attacked by giant leeches that live in the swamp where the team has to train because there's no swimming pool!"

"Arlo, this is a civilized place. I'm sure they have..."

"And I bet the kids there are all weird," I continued, "because they've grown up watching *Gilligan's Island* reruns, eating hamburgers with cigarette butts in them, sitting in snow for eleven and a half months a year and swimming in swamps infested with giant leeches! And they're probably all so weird that I won't want to be friends with any of them! In fact..."

"Arlo! Stop talking such nonsense! I'm sure you'll make lots of friends in your new school."

"Don't count on it, Mom," I said. "The only way I'll have friends in East Bend is if Zack and Bo sneaked into the trunk of the car when you weren't looking."

No matter what I said, Mom never did turn the car around. I guess it's been too long since she was a kid for her to understand that moving to a new town, going to a new school and taking me away from my friends were just about the worst things she could ever do to me.

"I have a new job to go to, Arlo," she kept telling me, as if that made up for lousy TV, lousy fast food, lousy swimming, and no Zack and Bo. "It'll be tough at first, but in the long run, things will be better for us."

I knew she was wrong.

When we finally arrived in East Bend, it wasn't as bad as I thought it would be. It was worse.

The walls of snow along the side of the road were so high, it felt like we were in a gigantic bobsled run.

And I was right—the only fast-food place in town was an old trailer called Bubba's Drive-in. Their specialty was the Bubba Burger. Between those two all-beef patties, I was sure Bubba put in a layer of cigarette butts.

The swimming pool was only open in July and August, and then only if it got warm enough. And the old farmhouse we rented had an old TV with a mangled antenna that only got two channels. One of them was all in French, and the other was so fuzzy it may as well have been broadcast from the North Pole. But the worst thing of all was that Zack and Bo weren't in the trunk of our car. I didn't have one single friend in East Bend. And going to school wasn't going to change anything. Anyone who lived in this dump of a town just had to be weird.

We arrived on a Sunday night, and Mom didn't want me to waste any time starting at my new school. There was only one elementary school in town—East Bend Elementary. How original!

On Monday morning, I rolled out of bed and remembered a little too late that I was sleeping on a top bunk. In the kitchen, the toast got stuck in the toaster and filled the house with smoke and set off the smoke alarm. In the bathroom, I got the hairbrush stuck in my hair and my mom had to cut it out. Great! On my first day at my new school,

I'd be the only kid in my class with a bald spot. After brushing my teeth with Mom's face cream, I accidentally flushed her favorite earrings down the toilet. All in all, it was a terrible start to what I knew was going to be a very bad day.

When Mom and I left the house for school, it felt like we were stepping into a giant deep freeze. I'd never gotten so cold so quickly. It was so cold I thought my eyeballs were going to freeze solid and roll out of their sockets. "I-i-it…n-n-never…g-g-gets this…c-c-cold in Vict-t-toria," I stuttered.

"Just a brisk February morning," Mom said, but her teeth were chattering like a row of tap-dancing chipmunks.

Our car didn't like the cold either. When Mom turned the key to start the engine, nothing happened. The car was frozen solid, just like me.

Mom went to the neighbors for help, and they let us borrow their pickup truck. I've already told you about my illustrious arrival at school in the pickup truck we borrowed from our neighbor, Fast Eddy of Fast Eddy's Manure Sales fame. My first day in East Bend was going downhill with every passing minute. But hold on. It only got worse.

CHAPTER 2

Mom and I sat in the manure truck in front of the school with a huge crowd of people staring at us. While Mom fought with the door handle to try and get her door open, I kept trying to convince her that going to this new school was a bad idea. I was desperate, so I grabbed the first idea that popped into my head and fed it to her.

"I don't need to go to this school, Mom. When I grow up, I'm going to be a sword swallower in the circus. Who needs to know how to read and write when you're swallowing swords?"

Mom just grunted and went on tugging at the door handle. She didn't bother trying my door, since it was held shut with a few meters of duct tape.

One of my mottos is "If at first you don't succeed, get more ridiculous." So that's what I did.

"And what happens if there's some strange disease going around at this school? And what happens if I catch it and my ears grow really huge? And what happens when it's class picture day? Do you want to send Grandma and Grandpa a picture of their grandson with elephant ears?"

Mom didn't seem to be paying any attention to me. She was too busy banging the door handle with her foot. While she was whaling away at the door, the school bell rang and all the kids obediently filed inside.

By the time Mom managed to kick her door open, the front of the school was deserted. At least there wasn't a crowd of gawkers anymore. On the other hand, I was going to be late on my first day at this new school, and they probably had a special punishment for anyone who was late.

Even though I hadn't set one foot in that school, I already hated it.

Just as I thought. The school was a complete dump. "It's probably a converted pig barn," I mumbled to Mom, even though I'd never actually been in a pig barn.

"I'm sure the school's got plenty of history" was all she said. In other words, she thought it was a dump too.

As we walked into the office, we were met by a man who looked like Santa Claus. For a minute, I figured maybe Mom had taken a wrong turn on the way from Victoria and we'd ended up at the North Pole. It sure felt cold enough.

Turns out that this guy was the principal, and his name was Mr. Butterworth. He led Mom and me into his office, acting really friendly. Immediately, I was suspicious. I'd seen adults act like this before. As long as your parents are around, they're the nicest, kindest, sweetest people on earth. But as soon as your parents leave... *POW*! They turn into snarly tyrants.

He asked Mom a million questions and filled in a long form, laughing and joking around, acting like he was really nice.

But I knew better. I knew that as soon as Mom left, he'd probably start yelling at me because I was late and assign me to snow-shoveling duty. He'd hand me a teaspoon and tell me to shovel every flake of snow off the back field! I hated snow. At least in Victoria, they couldn't order you to shovel rain.

When the forms were all filled out, Mom stood up to leave. She gave me a gentle hug, but I hugged back three times as hard, thinking, "Don't leave me with this maniac in this horrible converted pig barn with all these weirdo kids! Don't leave me, Mom! You're my only hope for survival!"

But Mom pried my arms off her shoulders, gently patted me on the head and said, "I'm sure you're going to enjoy your new school, Arlo. I'll pick you up after school, and we can go to the drive-in and grab a milkshake. How's that sound?"

Mom's voice broke a little, like there was something caught in her throat. I had a feeling she didn't want to leave me there. Maybe the truth of this horrible situation had finally sunk in. Maybe Mom was having second thoughts about moving here. Maybe she'd finally realized I was right about East Bend. Maybe, maybe, maybe. But it didn't matter, because she gave me a final wave and was out the door, on her way to the first day of her brand-new job.

I was left sitting in a small yellow plastic chair in the principal's office, waiting for Mr. Butterworth to transform from a jolly, roly-poly principal into a vile humungoid terror.

I waited. And I waited. But Mr. Butterworth didn't change one bit. He didn't yell at me for being late, and he didn't assign me to snow-shoveling duty.

He just smiled down at me and said, "I know starting out at a new school in the middle of the year can be tough, Arlo. But just give it a bit of time, and you'll really get to like our school."

Mr. Butterworth took me on a tour of the school, showing me the library, the gym and the washrooms. He seemed proud of the school, even though I still thought it looked like a converted pig barn.

Stopping at a classroom door, he said, "And we finish our tour of the school by arriving at your new classroom." As Mr. Butterworth was about to open the door, my gut began to churn as if the burnt toast I had eaten for breakfast had grown legs and was trying to jump back out. The thought of coming face-to-face with my new classmates made me feel like throwing up. But I knew I couldn't throw up right here! Throwing up at the door of the classroom would not make a good first impression.

As the door to the classroom swung open, twenty-five heads turned and fifty eyes stared right at me. I didn't stare back. Instead I stared at the top of my shoes. My stomach was still in explosion mode.

The principal introduced me to my new teacher. "Mrs. Armstrong. This is Arlo Billingsly…"

I didn't look up at my new teacher. Instead I turned to the principal and said, "I don't feel too…" I never finished my sentence. There was nothing I could do. Maybe it was the burnt toast. Maybe it was the fumes from the manure truck. Maybe it was just plain nerves. Whatever it was, I couldn't stop it.

Most of it landed on Mr. Butterworth's shoes. I thought being late for school was bad enough, but now I'd thrown up on the principal. He'd probably make me write lines for the rest of my life! "*I will not throw up on the principal's shoes ever again. I will not throw up on the principal's shoes ever again. I will not…*"

But instead of being concerned about his shoes being covered in barf, Mr. Butterworth seemed more concerned about me. He whisked me off to the staff washroom, where he gave me a washcloth and some mouthwash. After I'd gotten all the barf taste out of my mouth, I croaked, "Sorry."

"That's okay, Arlo," Mr. Butterworth said as he cleaned his shoes off with a paper towel. "You couldn't help it. Do you feel better?"

I nodded. It was a lie. I still felt lousy, but at least my stomach was empty.

He took me back to my new classroom. On the way, we passed the janitor in the hallway with a bucket and mop. I stared at the floor as he walked by.

Once again I stood outside the door of my new class-room. If I thought the first introduction to my new class had been tough, how could I face them now? You know how important first impressions are. Mine wasn't exactly spectacular. The kids in the class had probably already nicknamed me Barfy or Pukey or Upchuck or something even worse. But I didn't have much of a choice. Mr. Butterworth introduced me once again to my teacher. "Arlo, this is Mrs. Armstrong."

I still stared at my shoes. I wished I was back in my old class with my old teacher, Mrs. Peachly. She may have been old, but she was gentle and kind. Plus, I had never barfed in Mrs. Peachly's class.

"Hey there, Arlo!" my new teacher said. She didn't sound gentle, kind or even old. She sounded like a cheer-leader. I looked up from my shoes. Way up! Mrs. Armstrong was the tallest person I had ever met. At first I thought she was standing on stilts, but her legs looked like the real thing.

Along with being tall, Mrs. Armstrong had the widest smile in the universe. Her mouth was wide enough to slide a double-deluxe king-sized pizza in sideways.

The other strange thing about my new teacher was

her hair. It was wild. I mean, really wild. It looked like a man-eating plant from the Amazon rain forest. What else can you expect from a place like this, I thought. Weird schools have weird teachers.

"Hey, everyone! I'd like you to meet our newest class member—Mr. Arlo Billingsly!"

There was silence. I glanced really quickly around the class. Just as I thought. Every one of them was staring right back at me. I couldn't stand it, so I looked down at my shoes again.

"Would anyone like to stand up and officially welcome Arlo to our class?" Mrs. Armstrong asked. Not a peep from anyone. Finally a girl near the back of the room put up her hand. She looked like she could play middle line-backer for the B.C. Lions. Her arms were thicker than my waist. Even though she had two black pigtails sticking out from the sides of her head and wore a frilly pink dress, I could see by her steel-toed work boots that you wouldn't want to mess with her.

"Yes, Elsa," Mrs. Armstrong called. "Go ahead."

The girl stood up. "We're all glad to have you in our class, even if you do come to school in a manure truck and barf in the doorway," she said, adding a deep husky chuckle. I heard a bunch of other kids giggle and snicker. Mrs. Armstrong gave Elsa a dirty look as she sat down with a smug look on her face.

Another kid stood up, a boy this time. "Yes, Chuck. What do you have to say to Arlo?" Mrs. Armstrong said, giving Chuck a look that said, "Be nice, or else!"

Chuck had a huge black and blue bruise on his cheek, and his lower lip was about three times its proper size. It looked like he'd lost an argument with a gorilla. Then again, he was pretty tough-looking, so maybe the gorilla wasn't in such hot shape either.

"Yeah, we think...um...it's great to have you...um... in our class. We've never had anyone...um...in our class with a bald spot before!" Chuck sat down amid more giggling. This time it was louder.

"Now, everyone! Enough of that! Let's make Arlo feel welcome!"

Most of the kids were hunched over their desks, snickering and giggling behind folded arms and cupped hands. Most, that is, except for this skinny gawky kid who stumbled up the aisle from the back of the room, walking like a robot that needed its joints oiled.

The way he was bumping into desks and chairs made me wonder how good his eyesight was. He wore glasses with dark square frames; the lenses magnified his eyes so he looked like a bug. He stopped about one meter in front of me, holding out a bony hand at the end of a pale willowy arm.

I hesitated but finally reached out to shake his hand. His grip was so weak, for a second I was worried that I might crush his hand. We stood there shaking hands, and he wouldn't let go. Taking a deep breath, he said, in a voice that reminded me of my one and only violin lesson,

"Please excuse the rudeness of my fellow classmates, Arlo Billingsly. Personally, I would like to welcome you to our class and our school. I hope the remainder of the year will offer you a richly rewarding educational experience."

I didn't know what to say. No one had ever told me to have a "richly rewarding educational experience" before. I didn't even know what that was, so I didn't say anything. I just nodded, let go of his hand and stared back down at the tops of my shoes.

"Thank you so much, Cedric." Mrs. Armstrong beamed. "That was a lovely thing to say. And I'm sure, deep down inside, every single person in this class feels exactly the same way!"

Not likely. Mrs. Armstrong could say whatever she liked. I knew everyone in this class hated me. And already I hated everyone in this class. I hated the whole school. I hated the whole town. And I especially hated Mom for making me move here!

Maybe at recess I would jump over the fence and hitchhike back to Victoria.

CHapTER 3

M rs. Armstrong put me in an empty desk near the back of the room. Luckily, Elsa and Chuck weren't sitting close by. Neither was that strange kid named Cedric.

In the desk next to me was a girl wearing a Boston Bruins hockey jersey that hung down to her knees. I noticed she had some stitches on her chin, and when she smiled there was a gap where one of her front teeth should have been.

The girl leaned over and whispered, "*Psst*! What position do you play?"

"Huh?" I had no idea what she was talking about.

"In hockey! What position do you play?" the girl persisted.

"I don't know," I whispered back. In Victoria, when my friends and I played road hockey at recess, we never played positions.

"You're coming out to play with us at recess, aren't you? Our team can use all the help we can get! We really need a good defenseman," the girl said, still grinning that toothless grin.

"Cassie! Don't distract Arlo. Get back to work!" the teacher called. The girl shrugged her shoulders, turned back to her desk and pretended to work on some math questions.

For a second or two, I thought things might not be so bad around here. If they played road hockey, the kids weren't as weird as they looked. But who knows what their road hockey was like? Maybe they used old tree branches for sticks and frozen cow pies for the ball. Oh well. At least it would be close to the hockey I played. When the teacher wasn't looking, I leaned back over to Cassie.

"Sure. I'll play," I said. "But there's one problem. I don't have any equipment. My stick and gloves are in the moving van, and it doesn't get here until Wednesday."

"No problem!" Cassie said. "Mr. Butterworth has a couple of extra sticks and helmets in his office. I can lend you a pair of gloves, and we've got all kinds of skates left over from the skate swap. What size are you?"

"Skates?" I gasped. "Skates?"

"Well, what did you expect us to wear to play hockey? Golf shoes?" Cassie laughed.

"Where's the arena?" I asked. "I didn't see one when we drove in."

"An arena? I only wish! We skate on the swamp behind the school. During the winter, we have the biggest skating rink of any elementary school in the world!"

My stomach twisted into a knot. We played *road* hockey in Victoria. You play road hockey on a *road*. Not on ice. Some kids I knew wore in-line skates, but my friends and I just wore runners and pretended to skate. I was the greatest pretend skater in Canada. But this didn't sound like pretend. This was real skating with real skates on real ice!

If I went out at recess and tried to play real hockey on real skates, I would make a total fool of myself. It would be worse than barfing on the principal's shoes. When I flipped and flopped all over the ice, everyone in the school would know I was the only kid in Canada who couldn't skate. They'd laugh their guts out. I'd be the biggest joke of the year! I had to make up an excuse.

"I'd like to play, but I've got a sore knee. The doctor says I have to stay off it for another week."

"Oh, really?" Cassie said. "How did you hurt it?"

"I injured it bowling." It was the first idea that popped into my mind. I realized that the first idea is not always the best idea.

Cassie looked a little puzzled and said, "I've never heard of anyone getting injured bowling, unless they dropped the ball on their foot. But a knee injury?"

"Well...we...ah...in Victoria we have different rules for bowling. We allow body checking."

"Body checking? In bowling?" Cassie looked even more puzzled now.

"Yeah. It's an up-and-coming sport. But it's really rough," I said.

"Yeah, it must be," she said, nodding slowly.

"Cassie!" Mrs. Armstrong shouted. "I shouldn't have to keep reminding you! Back to work!"

Mrs. Armstrong put me to work right away. It looked like she was going to be a real slave driver. I got out my math notebook and started to do the questions written on the board. It was stuff I'd already done in Mrs. Peachly's class, so it was pretty easy.

In a while, the recess bell rang. The class stampeded out like a herd of buffalo. Everyone dove into a huge dog pile, fighting for coats, hats, hockey sticks, gloves, skates, helmets and scarves. In about one minute, everyone had disappeared out the door, and the room was empty. Empty, that is, except for me and that kid Cedric, who hadn't grabbed any hockey equipment. He just bundled himself up in so many layers of jackets, scarves and hats that he looked like a beach ball.

"You be careful out there, Cedric," Mrs. Armstrong said sweetly.

"Thank you for showing so much concern, Mrs. Armstrong. You are an exceptional human being," Cedric replied in his squawky voice. "But may I remind you of the note I placed upon the upper right-hand corner of your desk this morning?"

"Oh, I almost forgot! You'll be heading off to your doctor's appointment," the teacher replied, a little embarrassed.

"That's right, Mrs. Armstrong. Today it's more allergy tests. The doctor is hoping to narrow down which environmental stimuli trigger my plethora of allergic reactions. I'll get back to class as soon as I can."

Cedric shuffled out the door, leaving me alone in the room with Mrs. Armstrong. There was not a chance I'd head outside for recess when it was this cold. I was happy to stay in the warm classroom, so I kept working on the math assignment.

"Everyone out at recess, Arlo!" Mrs. Armstrong called. Was she serious? She was forcing me out into the cold? Did she want my delicate brain tissue to freeze? I was lousy at math already, but freeze half my brain and I'd have trouble counting past ten! "Out you go!" she repeated, closing my book and pulling out my chair. "Go and get some fresh air!" It looked like I didn't have a choice, so I put on every stitch of clothing I had and headed for the door.

The great outdoor rink Cassie had bragged about was just an overgrown frozen puddle. There was old plywood around the edges for boards, and a couple of goals had been made out of ancient pipes and netting.

When I got out there, kids were whirling around the rink at top speed, going in different directions. It looked like a demolition derby on ice, except no one was crashing. The main reason they didn't crash was that each and every one of them could skate. Some of them had wobbly ankles, but even they could turn both ways and stop before they smashed into the boards.

Most of them skated so fast they were like blurs across the ice. When they stopped, huge sprays of snow flew up from their blades like frozen tidal waves. I bet these kids were born on skates. I bet their first pair of baby booties had little blades on them, and they could skate before they walked. Instead of crawling around, they were skating backward and doing spinaramas. Guys like me who grew up wearing gumboots didn't stand a chance.

Mr. Butterworth was standing at center ice. He blew his whistle and dropped a puck. Swarms of kids chased the puck as it bounced around the rink. I couldn't tell who was on which team. I don't think it really mattered because when someone got the puck, they shot it at the nearest goal.

The goalies had copies of *National Geographic* tied to their shins with string. They each held a great big goalie stick cut out of plywood in one hand and a baseball mitt in the other.

A kid in a Toronto Maple Leafs jersey took the puck in the corner. He made three quick moves, leaving other kids sprawled on the ice. Right in front of the net, he whipped a low backhand shot. The puck deflected off the goalie's stick, went sailing over the boards and disappeared into a huge snowbank. All at once, everyone stopped and yelled, "ADIOS, MR. PUCK! WE'LL SEE YOU WITH THE DANDELIONS!"

Now I was certain that this was one weird school.

Mr. Butterworth pulled another puck out of his pocket and dropped it on the ice. A kid in a Chicago Black Hawks jersey took the puck and started stickhandling down the ice. He was doing really well until he caught an edge and went down. The puck bounced right to Cassie. She took a wild swing and slapped the puck at the goal. The shot was so hard it tore the first ten pages off the goalie's leg pad. The puck bounced off a goalpost and slid into the net.

Cassie raised her stick, cheering like she'd just scored a Stanley Cup-winning goal. Then she skated over to the side of the rink and yelled, "Hey, Arlo! You should be out here! Forget about that bowling injury! You've got to play hurt! This is way too much fun to miss!"

I nuzzled my face down into my jacket, trying to disappear. There was no chance they'd get me out on the ice. I'd be flopping around like a beached beluga whale. They'd probably use me as a human puck for slap shot practice.

I watched a bit more of the game, but it was about as exciting as watching the tumble dryer at the Laundromat. And not as warm. My legs were getting cold and tired from standing. It seemed like the longest recess in history.

I looked around for a place to sit, and I spotted the Dumpster, which looked like a good out-of-the-way spot where Cassie couldn't pester me with any more questions about my fake injuries. Shuffling over on my numb feet, I scrambled up onto the Dumpster's lid and sat with my feet dangling over the edge. Up this high, I had a pretty good view of the hockey game.

I watched the puck fly from stick to stick like it was in a pinball machine. Kids were crashing into the boards, into the net and into each other. My mom would have described the game as "organized chaos." I wasn't so sure about the "organized" part.

The bell for recess finally rang as Mr. Butterworth was untangling two kids from the net. I didn't feel like talking to anyone, so I waited on the Dumpster lid for everyone else to go inside before I jumped down.

It took the kids forever to untie their skates, put on their winter boots and wander back to class. About every five seconds, Mr. Butterworth said, "Get a move on, kids. Hurry up now. Your teachers are waiting for you..."

When there were only three or four kids left outside, something very strange happened. The Dumpster lid moved. I was sure it did. Then I felt it move again. Now I was certain something inside the Dumpster was pushing up on the lid. After I felt it move a third time, something inside the Dumpster banged on the lid! There was no doubt. Something was in there, and it was trying to get out!

I knew this was a weird town, but this was more than weird. This was creepy! I hated to imagine what was in the Dumpster and why it wanted out. I'd seen street people in Victoria going through Dumpsters, rummaging for old pop cans or half-eaten hamburgers. But there was a big difference between rummaging through a Dumpster in Victoria and actually living inside a Dumpster in the freezing winter in this crummy little town.

Whatever was inside had to be ugly. I mean, really ugly. Bad breath that smelled like pig manure. Fingernails long enough to reach up your nostrils and poke you in the brain. Greeny yellowy slimy teeth that had never been brushed. Ever. Ears so full of dirt, plants were sprouting out. Bloodshot eyes that looked in two separate directions at once. Armpits that smelled like broken sewer pipes. Ugliness, smelliness, all kinds of contagious diseases. What else would you expect from something that survived on a diet of rotten lunches, old math worksheets, plastic wrappers, coffee grounds, apple cores, empty drink boxes, snotty tissues and other tasty morsels!

The way I figured it, if I jumped off the lid and tried to run away, the thing inside would probably escape from the Dumpster, chase me down and swallow me whole for a midmorning snack. But if I stayed on the lid, I could keep the beast trapped inside.

The thing kept banging and pushing on the lid. It sounded like it had at least six arms and legs…unless there was more than one of them! Maybe there was a whole herd of stinky, smelly, grouchy Dumpster beasts! There was no way I'd move off the lid now. So what if I had to spend the rest of my life here. I'd rather have a long life sitting on a Dumpster lid than a short one in the mouth of a Dumpster monster.

So I sat. And sat. And sat. The banging got louder, and the thing inside made noises that sounded almost human. But I still wasn't going to budge, even after the last kid had gone inside. I could see through the window that Mrs. Armstrong had started the next lesson.

It sure was cold out. It reminded me of stories my mom had told me about growing up in Saskatchewan. If you touched your tongue to a metal pipe, it would instantly freeze to the metal. You'd have to either rip your tongue off or wait for spring thaw. Sitting there on the metal Dumpster lid, I had a horrible thought. What would happen if my rear end froze to the metal lid? Knowing this school, they wouldn't let me wait until spring thaw, so they'd probably have to perform some sort of surgery. Imagine what Mom would think when she saw her son being hauled into the hospital with his rear end frozen to the lid of a Dumpster! I wondered if they could even fit a Dumpster lid in the operating room.

I snapped back to reality as the back door of the school swung open. Out came Mr. Butterworth. He was looking for something. Probably me.

What could I do? Jump off the lid, run around the school and go in another door? But then the thing in the Dumpster would escape and eat both Mr. Butterworth and me. On the other hand, maybe it would eat Mr. Butterworth first and then be too full to eat me.

"Arlo! Are you out here?" Mr. Butterworth called. I didn't think he'd seen me yet, even though he was walking in my general direction. Then a really strange thing happened. The beast in the Dumpster stopped making noise. It stopped pushing on the lid. It was quiet.

Mr. Butterworth came even closer. "Arlo! Are you out here!" he yelled again.

I debated whether to call out to Mr. Butterworth and tell him where I was. What would I say? Hey, Mr. Butterworth, I'm over here, sitting on this Dumpster lid so the beast inside won't escape and eat us.

For some reason, I didn't think he'd believe me. Especially now that the beast was quiet.

"Arlo? Where are you!" he called again. I could only think of one thing to do.

"I'm over here, Mr. Butterworth!" I yelled. "I can't move because my bum is frozen to the lid of the Dumpster!"

Mr. Butterworth lumbered toward me. "Your what?" he asked.

I pretended to try to lift myself off the Dumpster lid to show I couldn't budge. Then I quickly held my hand out to Mr. Butterworth and said, "Could you please give me a pull?"

The principal looked like he didn't know what I was talking about, but I wasn't about to explain. He grabbed my wrist.

"Now, pull!" I said. He pulled gently, and I launched myself off the Dumpster, through the air past Mr. Butterworth and into the snow. I hit the ground running at full speed, heading for the door of the school. If the thing from the Dumpster threw the lid open and burst out, I wasn't going to be around when it ate Mr. Butterworth in one gulp. "Thanks, Mr. Butterworth!" I yelled. "I'd better get going! I'm late for class and I don't want to miss anything!"

I didn't stop running until I got to the door of my classroom. Mrs. Armstrong said, "So there you are, Arlo. We were so worried! What happened to you?"

I couldn't tell Mrs. Armstrong and the whole class that I was late because my bum was frozen to the Dumpster lid. Forget it. I'd have to think of some other excuse.

"I was oiling the hinges on the Dumpster lid," I said. "I was the Dumpster monitor at my last school, so I thought I'd continue doing it here."

"Oh," Mrs. Armstrong said. "How...how kind of you." I had a feeling she didn't believe me.

chapter 4

After recess our class lined up and filed down to the gym for a school assembly. Mrs. Armstrong said it was a recognition assembly. I hate recognition assemblies. They always recognize kids who win bowling trophies, get first prize for their water safety poster or earn the most money selling lightbulbs for school fundraisers. They never recognize kids who can walk on the top of the safety railing all the way around the sewage treatment ponds or kids who can stuff two complete packages of bubble gum in their mouths and blow bubbles bigger than their heads. That's why I was never called up to the front at recognition assemblies. Adults only recognize stuff they think is important. Not the stuff I'm good at.

Each class sat in a row across the gym, with the kindergarten class at the front and the older kids at the back. Our class sat near the back, with the grade sevens right behind us. While I was waiting for the assembly to begin,

I overheard the conversation between the two boys behind me.

"Do you figure X will have enough time to get ready?" one kid said.

"Yeah, plenty of time."

"That sure was a close call at recess."

"I'll say it was. Old Butterball nearly had us."

"Yeah, he sure did. I don't know if the Dumpster's a very good place to hold our meetings anymore."

Hold their meetings? Could these two kids be the Dumpster monster—or what I thought was the Dumpster monster?

"The Dumpster's a perfect place to hold our meetings," the other kid said. "If it wasn't for that stupid kid sitting on the lid, there wouldn't have been a problem at recess."

"Yeah, you're right. What did Butterball call him?"

"It sounded like Arlo to me."

"Arlo?"

"Yeah, I'm pretty sure."

"What's an Arlo?"

"It's a kid's name, stupid."

"There's a kid in this school called Arlo? Who is he?"

"Beats me. But when I find out, he's gonna learn a lesson about Dumpster lids he'll never forget!"

I gulped.

Mr. Butterworth stood at the front of the assembly. "Before we begin our recognition assembly, I'd like you all to meet our newest student here at East Bend School!"

I wished I could shrink and disappear between the cracks in the floor. I was doomed. Those two thugs behind me would know I was the Arlo who sat on the Dumpster lid at recess. I figured if Mr. Butterworth introduced me to the school, I'd have about nine seconds to live.

"This new student comes to us all the way from our provincial capital, Victoria, British Columbia. His name is…" But before another syllable came from Mr. Butterworth's lips, the side doors of the gym flew open and a kid on a BMX bike burst in. He was dressed in baggy black clothing, and he had a bright orange ski mask over his face.

The kid zipped down to the far end of the gym. He whizzed around behind the grade sevens, bunny-hopped past the grade fours, and then he popped a wheelie right in front of the kindergarten class. The kids all whooped and screamed in a mixture of excitement and surprise.

By the way Mr. Butterworth and the teachers reacted, I could tell this wasn't part of the recognition assembly. This definitely wasn't the sort of behavior teachers liked to recognize. Mr. Butterworth's face turned red, and he shook his right hand as if he was going to shout, but nothing came out of his mouth except grunts and yells.

The only adult who came close to the kid on the bike was the grade seven teacher. He dove as the kid went past, but the masked cyclist changed direction just in time. The teacher sailed through the air and landed in the librarian's lap.

The kids kept up their wild screaming and yelling. A couple of the kindergarten kids were so excited they left little puddles on the gym floor.

The masked stunt rider rolled up to the back door of the gym, kicked it open and pedaled back outside again. He was gone as mysteriously as he had arrived, leaving nothing but a few tire marks on the floor, a bunch of wildly excited kids and a pack of angry teachers.

Mr. Butterworth was so flustered, he ended the assembly right then and there. I let out a huge sigh of relief. I had escaped Mr. Butterworth's introduction. And for now, I had escaped being introduced to the knuckle-dragging goons behind me.

Lunch was a lot like recess. Horrible. I didn't eat the sandwich Mom had packed. It tasted like she'd put one of my stinky old runners between two slices of stale bread. The cookies had been crushed into powder and the apple looked like it had been used by the Blue Jays for batting practice.

After eating lunch, we had a choice of going outside or joining the choir in the gym. The last time I had tried singing, I was nearly arrested by the police for disturbing the peace. Choir was not a good idea. I'd rather stand outside and go numb from the cold. To make sure Cassie didn't bug me about hockey again, I limped around to show my knee hadn't fully recovered from my bowling injury. I also stayed well away from the Dumpster.

Most of the kids were back out on the ice rink. It looked really dumb. All those kids chasing that little hunk of rubber, pretending they were playing in the NHL.

I was standing at one end of the rink when Cassie skated by yelling, "Hey, Arlo! How's the knee doing?"

"It's still pretty sore," I said, bending my knee slowly and wincing in imaginary pain.

"So this is Arlo," said a voice behind me. It was a slow sinister voice, the kind bad guys in movies always have.

"Yep. This is the guy," said another voice. I recognized those voices. They belonged to the two kids who sat behind me at the assembly. I had a feeling they wanted to talk to me about the Dumpster, but I didn't really want to talk to them. I just stood there, pretending to watch the hockey game.

"Hey, kid. I'm talking to you!" one of them snarled.

"Yeah, and so am I!…aren't I?" said the other.

"No, you're not, stupid! I'm the one doing the talking. You just stand there and try not to look too stupid."

"Are you sure?"

"That's what X said. And what X says goes."

While these two guys argued, I thought I'd make a run for it, but then Cassie would see that my bowling injury was fake. Besides, where was there to run? I turned around to face the two stooges.

One kid was about as tall as me but three times wider. He had a goofy leather hat with flaps of fur sticking out on the sides like little wings. His fat cheeks jiggled as he chomped on a big wad of gum. The guy beside him looked like a flagpole without a flag. He wore a really long baggy hoodie with the hood pulled tightly around his face. All you could see was a huge beak of a nose poking out of the hood, and two little eyes that blinked really fast.

"So, this is Arlo, is it?" said the fat one again.

"Arlo? Arlo?" said the skinny one. "What kind of a name is that?"

"Sounds like something that grows under your toenails!"

"Yeah. Sort of like athlete's toe!"

The fat kid glared at the skinny one and said, "Yeah, except worse. Arlo-itis."

"Hey! I think my grandma had that! She had to walk with a cane, and she even had to give up going to Bingo and…"

"Shut up, Rocko! You talk too much! Not to mention your other problem."

"What's that, Pinball?"

"You're stupid, Rocko! You're stupid!" The fat one named Pinball turned to me. "You're new here, right?"

I nodded.

"Don't know much about the school, do you?"

I shrugged my shoulders.

"So you haven't met X yet."

I shook my head.

"Well, consider this your lucky day." Pinball chuckled. "X wants to have a word with you. In his office. Pronto."

X? Who was X? I'd never heard of anyone whose name started with X. Maybe his full name was X-ray. Or maybe Xylophone. Or Xerxes. Whatever it was, it had to be unusual. And he had his own office? I didn't think this school could get any stranger, but it kept surprising me.

"Look, kid. No one keeps X waiting. You're coming with us, or me and Rocko here will have to use some gentle persuasion...if you know what I mean."

"Yeah! Pinball's right!" Rocko said. "You move along and nothing gets busted, you hear?"

I had trouble seeing Rocko breaking anything, except maybe his own nose. I could probably snap Rocko in two with one of my feeble karate chops.

Snapping Pinball in two was a different story, but at least I could easily outrun him. He looked about as fast as a three-legged elephant. I could run away if I wanted, but then these guys would be after me every lunch and recess and probably after school until they finally caught up with me.

And then there was X, whoever he was. He was probably some mega-muscle bodybuilder armed with a bazooka. I decided the safest thing to do was cooperate.

ChAPTER 5

I soon learned the location of X's office. It was the Dumpster. I should have known.

Rocko held the lid open. He grinned, and I noticed a huge gap where his front teeth should have been. "After you," he said, giving me a shove.

Like most people, I'd never been inside a Dumpster before. Taking a tour of the inside of a Dumpster has never been on my top ten list of things to do. But here I was, climbing up the side of this huge metal box, swinging my legs over into the darkness. After a short free fall, I landed in a pile of garbage bags full of...well...garbage. Stinky garbage. Rocko and Pinball landed in the Dumpster beside me.

The lid banged shut and everything went black. Pitch-black. I couldn't see my hand in front of my nose. I couldn't even see my nose. As offices go, X's office was the darkest, smelliest office I'd ever been in. I guess it could have been worse. At least most of the garbage from schools is wrapped in bags and doesn't smell too nasty. It might be different if this was a Dumpster outside, say, a fish-gutting factory. In this inky darkness, a light suddenly appeared at the far end of the Dumpster. The light shone right in my eyes, so I still couldn't see anything.

"X, this is Arlo," Pinball said. "I brought him here, just like you told me to."

"I helped too, X! I really did!" Rocko said.

"Yeah, right! All you did was stand around and think you were acting tough! You're about as tough as two-week-old Jell-O!" Pinball snarled.

"Oh yeah?"

"Yeah!"

"ENOUGH!" X said. His voice sounded really strange—growly, scratchy and whiny, all at the same time. But as strange as his voice was, it still made Rocko and Pinball shut up right away. They seemed pretty obedient. Maybe they were really afraid of this X.

"Why aren't you playing hockey like everyone else?" X said, the words slowly oozing out of his mouth.

"Sore shoulder," I said. I figured that maybe X was some sort of secret agent who dealt with anyone who didn't play hockey. Just to be on the safe side, I lied again. "I hurt my shoulder white-water rafting last week. Doctor says not to play hockey for a while."

"We hate hockey," X said. "We think anyone who plays hockey is a doofus. Hockey is a stupid waste of time."

"Yeah," Rocko piped up. "What a bunch of losers!"

"Worse than losers!" Pinball said. "They're low-down, good-for-nothing, pea-brained, puck-chasing bozos!"

"No! They're even worse than that!" Rocko piped up again. "I say they're dumb, stupid, idiot…"

"ENOUGH!" roared X again. Pinball and Rocko immediately shut up. "We choose to do things that are much more exciting…much more daring…much more dangerous than playing hockey," X said.

Now I knew who X was. "Daring things like riding your bike through a school assembly?" I asked.

"Yep! That's X!" Pinball yelled. "That was him all right!"

"SHUT UP!" snapped X.

"Yeah, shut up," Rocko added. "Do you want the whole world to know that X is the most wanted kid in this school?"

"No, you shut up, you big gallumph!" Pinball barked back. "Your mouth's so big, they could use it for a McDonald's drive-thru!"

"Ah, shut up!"

"Shut up yourself!"

"ENOUGH!" There was silence. "You, Arlo, are honored to be in the presence of the only three members of the Dumpster Dudes."

"Yeah! That's us!" Rocko shouted. "The Dumpster Dudes!! Me, X and Pinball!"

"Would you shut your mouth before I tie your tongue into a granny knot!" Pinball yelled.

X went on in that same slow strange voice. "To become one of us, you must hate hockey, baseball, basketball and all those boring sports that everyone else in the school wastes their time playing."

"That sounds like me," I said, even though I wasn't sure I wanted to join these guys, no matter how much they hated hockey. I figured it wasn't the best time to mention that I actually played soccer and baseball.

"That's only part of why we have this exclusive group," X said. "Instead of those stupid games, we do things that most people only dream—or have nightmares—about. So the chance to become one of us is a rare opportunity, especially for someone new to our school. Consider yourself lucky."

I wasn't exactly sure if this was my idea of "lucky," but I croaked, "Thanks," anyway.

"We don't let just anyone become a member," X said. "To become one of us, you must pass a test."

"A test? What sort of test?" I said, hoping it didn't have anything to do with double-digit multiplication.

"It's like a dare. A dangerous stunt. We tell you what you must do. If you succeed, you become one of us. You become one of the select few—a lifetime member of the Dumpster Dudes."

"Yeah! Lifetime! That's like...until you die or move to South America or something!" Rocko said proudly.

"Shut up, Rocko!" Pinball barked. "Don't interrupt X!"

"As a member, you can take part in the most daring and dangerous stunts ever seen in a school anywhere in the world! You think today's stunt was spectacular? Just wait until you see what we have planned!"

I had to admit that when X came into the gym on his bike, it was the craziest, strangest and probably greatest thing I'd ever seen at an assembly. It was even better than the time at my old school when a juggler accidentally lit his hair on fire.

"Of course, becoming a Dumpster Dude is your decision," X continued. "If you want to become one of us, we'll meet here tomorrow at recess. But if you don't want to join...I guess you'll just have to face the consequences..."

The light clicked off.

I heard a thump on the lid of the Dumpster.

"Ouch!" It was Rocko.

"How many times do I have to tell you?" Pinball said. "You never stand up in a Dumpster! Everyone knows that!"

"Ah, shut up!" Rocko said, pushing open the lid. Pinball grabbed me by the back of my jacket and gave me a heave. I rolled over the edge of the Dumpster and tumbled outside into the snow. The lid slammed shut, and all I heard was, "Ouch! Hey, you pinhead! Watch my fingers next time!"

"Why should I? They're not my fingers. And besides,

they're the ugliest fingers I've ever seen. Even the Elephant Man's fingers weren't as ugly as yours!"

"Oh yeah?"

"Yeah!"

As I walked back to class, I thought about the Dumpster Dudes. Who was X, anyway? Did he go to this school? Or did he just hang out in the Dumpster? Was he a kid at all? Maybe X was a wanted criminal! That's why he couldn't use his real name. Maybe he robbed a bank and bought the Dumpster with the money and had it put at the school so he could lure kids like me into a life of crime. Or maybe X was an alien! Maybe the Dumpster was actually a disguised alien spacecraft! Maybe X was just a disembodied head! Maybe the Dumpster Dudes were alien life-forms planning to colonize the Earth.

All I knew was that if I didn't agree to join the Dumpster Dudes, I'd have to face the consequences. I didn't exactly know what that meant, but it didn't sound good. Even though X hadn't mentioned how I sat on the Dumpster lid at recess, I knew he was mad about it. It was a kind of silent threat. If I didn't join their group, they'd probably do stuff like drop live snakes down the back of my pants or hide jalapeno peppers in my sandwiches. Or maybe they'd just simply beat the tar out of me. Flatten my nose, knock a few teeth out, twist my arm so it nearly breaks loose, pull clumps of hair out of my head...standard bully stuff.

On the other hand, if I did join the club, who knows what they'd make me do as my test? And what if I got caught doing something really stupid? I couldn't ride a bike through the gym. I'd probably crash into the wall or get a flat tire. Or maybe the chain would fall off. Then Mr. Butterworth would dive on me and pin me to the ground, squishing me with his two hundred kilos of principalship. And then Mom would be called in, and I'd be grounded for the rest of my life. Plus, everyone in the school would point at me and say, "There's that kid who tried to ride his bike in the assembly, but he got his pants caught in the chain and crashed into the kindergarten class! What a dummy!"

Maybe joining the choir wasn't such a bad idea after all.

CHAPTER 6

B ack in class after lunch, all anyone could talk about was the great plays they had made in the hockey game.

"Did you see the move I put on the goalie?" said a kid with a big bruise on his cheek. "I deked him right out of his underwear!" The kid didn't say how he got the bruise on his cheek, but I bet it was from running into a goalpost or getting the butt end of someone's stick.

"Lori, Nora and I should be called 'The Trio of Doom,'" a girl with red hair and braces boasted. "We passed the puck around like it was magnetized to our sticks! Anyone who tried to stop us was doomed."

"Hey, Arlo!" It was Cassie. "You missed a great game! We stomped 'em eight to three. I had a goal and three assists! I named myself the first star of the game!" she said, holding her hands up triumphantly. "How's your knee? I saw you running in after lunch and it didn't seem so bad." Cassie gave me a suspicious look, put her hands on her hips and waited for an answer.

"Oh…well…it only bothers me when I skate," I babbled, scrambling for a reply she might believe.

"Hmm. That's weird," she replied.

"Yeah. The doctor said it's a pretty rare injury, and I may have to have a knee transplant."

"Wow!" Cassie said. "I hope you get it done soon so you can get back on the ice."

"They're looking around for a knee donor, but right now, the only one they can find is a penguin. I just hope they find a replacement before it's too late…"

I hated having to make these stories up all the time, just so I wouldn't look stupid. At least with the Dumpster Dudes, I wouldn't have to pretend I hated skating. Then again, would I rather be forced to do one of their dangerous stunts? I still wasn't sure.

That afternoon in class, I was too busy thinking about the Dumpster Dudes to pay much attention. When I don't pay attention, I do stupid things. Like when Mrs. Armstrong asked me to write a spelling word on some chart paper, I accidentally walked up to the front of the room and wrote the word with my purple glue stick.

When Mrs. Armstrong told me to feed the class's pet hamster, I left the cage door open and it escaped. We spent half the afternoon trying to get him out of an air vent in the wall.

The worst thing of all happened during art class when we were painting. Don't ask me why I did it. Maybe I was thirsty. Maybe I just wasn't thinking. Maybe it was a bit of both. I picked up the cup of water we were using to clean the brushes and *glug...glug...glug...*I drank it right to the last drop.

"EEEOW! Gross! Arlo drank the dirty paint water!" Elsa screamed.

"Arlo! What in the world are you doing?" Mrs. Armstrong yelled across the room.

"It's okay," I said. "I drink dirty paint water all the time! It's...it's actually very good for you! It's full of vitamin C! Prevents bad breath, gets rid of dandruff! Kids in Bolivia have to drink three cups of dirty paint water a day!"

I looked around the class. Everyone was staring. I don't think anyone believed me, but I smiled anyway.

"Grooooooooss!" some kid groaned.

"His tongue and teeth are all purple!" Chuck shouted.

"Gross me out!" Elsa said. "You better watch out. The next thing you know, he'll be eating out of the garbage can."

"I think he already has," Chuck sneered. "At least he smells like he has."

"Drinking paint water is an honest mistake," a voice screeched from the back of the room, and everyone knew right away who it was. It was that little guy, Cedric. "Rather than criticize him, I think we should understand that Arlo is experiencing a very difficult, anxiety-creating day, this being his first day in a new school. Rather than criticize, we should empathize!"

"Whatever that means," Chuck grumbled under his breath.

"Cedric is absolutely right!" Mrs. Armstrong declared. "And for those of you who don't know what empathy is, it means putting yourself in that person's place and trying to understand how they are feeling. So let's all try to have a bit more empathy for Arlo."

I knew by the darting eyes and the snickers behind covered mouths that no one really cared much about empathy. After only one day in my new class, I was known as the kid who arrived at school in a manure truck, barfed on the principal's shoes, wrote in glue on chart paper and drank dirty paint water. Everyone thought I was a wacko goony freak. And they hadn't even seen me skate yet!

But doing weird stuff didn't seem to bother X, Pinball and Rocko. They actually liked doing things like riding a bike through a school assembly. They didn't care what anyone else thought. If I was a member of the Dumpster Dudes, I wouldn't have to worry about being weird. I wouldn't have to worry about what all the goofs in my class thought of me. All that would matter was the Dumpster Dudes.

Maybe joining wasn't such a bad idea after all.

The end of the day finally arrived. They say that time flies when you're having fun, and now I know for sure that the opposite is also true. It felt like the school day had been seventy-two hours long.

I was waiting in front of the school for Mom to pick me up. Around the corner came the banging, rattling truck with *Fast Eddy's Manure Sales* written on the side. The whole school was out there to see my mom pick me up in the world's ugliest truck. I was so embarrassed, I looked for a rock to crawl under, but all the rocks were buried under mountains of snow. Maybe I should have dug a hole in the snow and crawled in.

A little kid tugged at my jacket and said, "Your mom sells manure? My dad sells furniture. It doesn't smell so bad."

Mom had finally gotten the hang of opening her door. With one swift kick, the driver's side door flew open. She stepped out to let me in. As I climbed into the truck, Cassie waved from the bus lineup and yelled, "Hope your knee gets better soon, Arlo!" I slid across the seat to the passenger side, keeping my head down and ignoring her as best I could.

Mom gave me a worried look and said, "Do you have a problem with your knee, Arlo?"

"No, my knee's fine," I said. "She must be talking to another Arlo."

"There's another Arlo at this school?"

"Oh yeah," I said. "There's three or four Arlos.

I'm not sure which one has the bad knee."

"Oh," Mom said. She always just said "Oh" when she didn't believe me. Lately, she'd been saying "Oh" a lot.

As we pulled out of the parking lot, Mom asked, with fake enthusiasm, "So, tell me all about your first day. I'm dying to hear about your new school!"

After the most horrible day of my life, I wasn't going to make it easy for Mom. After all, being in this dumpy town and going to this awful school was all her fault. I didn't say a word. I just snorted and looked out the window.

"Did you make some new friends?" she asked, sounding as cheerful as ever.

I snorted again. I could snort all day. Mom could say whatever she wanted, but I would just snort.

"What's your new teacher like?" Mom tried to keep up the enthusiasm, but I could tell she was losing it.

"Do you want to hear about my first day at work, Arlo?"

I snorted again, even though I was a little curious about how Mom liked her new job. I was kind of hoping her first day had been as bad as mine. Maybe she'd decide to quit and move us back to Victoria. But I figured by the tone of her voice and the way she asked the question, her job must be okay. In fact, she probably liked it. She probably had fun. She probably met some nice, friendly, normal people.

After I hadn't replied to her third question in a row, Mom let out a long sigh and said, "Why don't you and I go down to that drive-in and get ourselves a couple of milkshakes?"

"The kids at school warned me about getting milkshakes here in the winter," I replied in a deadpan voice. "They say the guy at the drive-in puts antifreeze in the milkshakes so they won't freeze solid."

Mom sighed, but she didn't give up. She was determined to pry a smile out of me. But there was no chance! There was only one way to cheer me up, and since Mom wasn't about to move back to Victoria, I figured I'd be frowning forever.

Mom pulled the truck over to the side of the road and rustled around under the seat. Finally she pulled out a plastic bag. "I've got something for you, Arlo. It's sort of a reward for surviving the first day at your new school." Handing the bag over to me, she said, "Go ahead. Take a look."

I opened the bag and took a peek inside. Then I screamed.

"Skates! You got me skates! Why do I need skates? Why couldn't you get me something I wanted, like a pet boa constrictor or a chain saw? Not skates!"

"Now, Arlo, calm down," she said. "You need skates. Everyone at work says the kids here all play ice hockey. If you want to make friends, you've got to learn to play ice hockey."

"But ice hockey's so...so...stupid! Why don't they

play a real game here like…like…full-contact bowling! Now that's a REAL game."

"Arlo, don't be ridiculous. Ice hockey's a great game."

"In case you didn't know, Mother, I've never skated before. I've never even had a pair of skates on my feet! How many times do I have to remind you that I'm the only kid in Canada who can't skate?"

"Now you're exaggerating, Arlo. I hate it when you exaggerate. I'm sure there are plenty of kids your age who don't know how to skate."

"Yeah, sure there are. And there's a name for them. They're called boneheaded klutzomaniacs! And everyone makes fun of them!"

"Arlo, you're a good athlete. You can learn to skate."

"Yeah, but in the meantime, I'll be East Bend School's version of Bongo the Clown. I'll be the biggest joke in the school!"

This was the last straw. My own mother buying me a pair of skates and forcing me to play ice hockey. It seemed like everyone around here was pushing me into this dumb sport just so I could look even dumber than I did already.

Enough was enough. I couldn't take any more. First Mrs. Armstrong, then Mr. Butterworth, Cassie, and now my own mother!

Tomorrow at recess, I'd meet X, Rocko and Pinball in the Dumpster. I'd find out what I had to do to become a Dumpster Dude. Anything would be better than lacing up those skates.

chapter 7

The next morning when the recess bell rang, I raced outside and headed straight for the Dumpster. I knocked on the lid, and it swung open. A chubby hand, which must have been Pinball's, reached out, grabbed me by the back of my jacket and pulled me inside. Tumbling into the Dumpster headfirst, my face landed in something mushy that tasted like papier-mâché paste. I remembered the taste from kindergarten.

In kindergarten, I ate a whole bucketful of papier-mâché paste because my former best friend, Vinnie, told me it would harden inside me and make me bulletproof, just like Superman. Even though I haven't eaten any papier-mâché paste since, I can still remember the taste. But wet, squooshy, sticky stuff is even more gross when you don't know what it is. Pinball put his hand in it. You could tell by the way he yelled, he didn't know what it was.

"Yeow! Ooooh! Gross! I think I just stuck my

hand in...in...old smushed brains!"

A light clicked on and shone in my eyes. X cleared his throat, and Pinball went from yowling and howling to whimpering.

Rocko wasn't there yet, but he announced his arrival soon with two knocks on the lid. Pinball shoved the lid open and Rocko dove in—right into the middle of the papier-mâché paste.

"Hey! This is great!" Rocko said, smacking his lips. "Someone threw some perfectly good oatmeal into the Dumpster. I love oatmeal! Mmm!"

"That's not oatmeal, you dunderhead!" Pinball screamed. "That's squished brains!"

"No, it's not. Squished brains don't taste this good," Rocko said between finger lickings.

I didn't ask him how he knew what squished brains tasted like. And I didn't tell him the oatmeal was really papier-mâché paste. I thought I'd wait until it dried inside him. Then I could tell him he was bulletproof.

"ENOUGH!" X barked from behind the flashlight. He spoke just like the last time—really slowly and in that strange growly, scratchy voice.

"So, you've decided to see if you've got what it takes to become a Dumpster Dude, have you?"

"Uh...ah...I...guess so," I answered. Now that I was face-to-face with X and waiting to hear what my test would be, joining them didn't seem as great an idea as it had ten minutes ago.

"Well, we'll soon see if you've got what it takes, won't we, boys?" X said.

"Yeah! Yeah! You're right, X! You betcha! Sure thing!" Rocko and Pinball babbled.

"It's as simple as this," X continued. "I will set you a test. If you succeed, you will become a lifetime member of the Dumpster Dudes. But if you fail..." He didn't finish the sentence. He didn't have to. I knew what he meant.

"Yeah!" Rocko said. "If you're a member, you can come to the Dumpster any time you want!"

Wow, I thought. A lifetime member.

"Can I just ask one teensy weensy question?" I said. "Why do you guys...er, I mean dudes, meet in the Dumpster?"

"You got a problem with the Dumpster?" Pinball said.

"No, not at all!" I replied. "I was just a little curious, that's all."

"Quite simple," X said. "No one ever bothers us in here. No one comes near us except the janitor who dumps the garbage from the school at night. The rest of the time, no one dares come near."

"Yeah! They're scaredy chickens!" Rocko said.

"It's scaredy cats, you lunkhead!" Pinball said.

"What about the big truck that comes to empty it?" I asked. I'd seen those gigantic trucks that lift Dumpsters up and empty the garbage into this huge compressor. I didn't like the idea of being dumped and compressed.

"We got inside information," Pinball said. "My uncle's friend's cousin drives the truck, so he tells me the pickup times. You scared or something?"

"No," I said, but it was a lie. I didn't really trust Pinball's inside information. But then again, maybe becoming a lifetime member of the Dumpster Dudes was worth the risk. Anything was better than playing hockey.

"Go ahead, X. Tell me what you want me to do. I'll do whatever you say," I said eagerly. Maybe a little too eagerly, as Rocko and Pinball snickered.

"Very well," X said. "Listen carefully. East Bend Elementary is an old school with a network of very large air ducts running through the ceilings. The hot air is blown through these ducts to vents in every room. This means that, from any room, it is possible to reach any other room in the school through the ducts. For your test, you will be required to enter the air ducts through a vent in the ceiling of the custodian's room, crawl through the ducts to the other end of the school and come out in the supply room."

Pinball chuckled. "Oooh, that's a good one, X!"

"Yeah," Rocko snickered. "That's one of my favorites, X!"

As I listened to the details of the test, at first I thought X was joking. "You can't be serious," I said with a feeble laugh.

"Oh, yes. I am very serious," X growled. "In fact, I'm more than serious!"

"You really want me to crawl through the air ducts?" I said.

X didn't say anything. He just moved the flashlight up and down like it was nodding.

"But what if I get stuck? I'll never get out! I'll be stuck up there forever until some archaeologist discovers my bones in about a thousand years! I'll be like that caveman they found frozen in a glacier. At least he got to be called the Ice Man. They'll probably call me something really dumb like the Air Duct Boy!"

"ENOUGH!" X growled. I was quiet. "It's been done before. This school has very large air ducts. There's plenty of room for you to crawl."

"Yeah, they're really big," Rocko said. "Even Pinball almost fits through."

"Shut up, ya stork!"

"Stork? Me? Then what are you? An overstuffed hippo?"

I didn't care how big the air ducts were. I didn't care if you could drive a tank through them. I was still worried about this stunt. "How am I supposed to get into the custodian's room? How am I supposed to find my way through all the ducts? What am I supposed to do when I get to the supply room?"

X spoke again. "We will provide you with everything you need. Meet us in the boys' washroom at one fifteen this afternoon. We will give you the rest of the details then. And if you don't show up...well...that's your choice."

Click went the light. X disappeared into darkness.

Pushing the Dumpster lid open, Pinball sneered. "See ya at one fifteen...or else!"

I felt stunned as I climbed out. X was definitely serious about me crawling through the air ducts in the ceiling. And Pinball was just as serious about the "or else" part if I chickened out. But then I asked myself, Would I rather be crawling around the air ducts or slithering around on the ice outside? Suddenly the air ducts didn't seem so bad.

As I headed toward the school, I wanted to make sure I didn't forget the meeting time, so I repeated, "One fifteen boys' washroom, one fifteen boys' washroom, one fifteen boys' washroom" under my breath. In the hallway on my way back to class, I passed Mrs. Armstrong. "Oh, Mrs. Armstrong!" I said.

"Yes, Arlo. What is it?" she said, grinning her toothy grin.

"At one fifteen this afternoon, I have to go to the washroom."

"Oh," she said, looking a little surprised. "You certainly plan ahead, don't you?"

Right after recess there was another assembly to make up for the one X interrupted the day before. Everyone in the school was buzzing, wondering if the mystery bike rider would strike again. Mr. Butterworth put a teacher at each door, just in case.

But I knew X wouldn't be doing anything at this assembly. There were only four of us in the school who knew what was going on. No one else had a clue. It was great having inside information.

One bit of information I didn't have, though, was the actual identity of the mysterious X. I took the opportunity at the assembly to look around, scanning the rows of kids, trying to figure out if one of them might be our leader. I spotted Rocko and Pinball, and they both gave me the thumbs-up sign and grinned their goofy grins. But sitting on either side of them were girls—one with curly, bright red hair, and the other with long, wavy, blond hair. From the sound of X's voice, neither of those girls could be the leader of the Dumpster Dudes.

My search for the real X was constantly interrupted by the person sitting next to me—Cassie. She was like a scrap of paper stuck to your finger with glue. No matter how hard you shook your hand, it wouldn't come off.

"You going to come out and play at lunch?" she asked.

I just shrugged my shoulders.

"It'll be great!" she said. "It's us against the teachers!" Her enthusiasm really bugged me. She made it sound so great when she talked about playing hockey, but I knew better.

A boy sitting next to Cassie said, "Yeah! It'll be great! I hear Mrs. Pendergast, the kindergarten teacher, is going in goal for the teachers. The word on her is shoot high to the stick side."

A girl sitting in front of us turned around. "And Mr. Birch is away for the rest of the week," she said. "We have Ms. Welch as our substitute teacher, and she had a tryout with the Canadian women's hockey team three years ago!"

"Yikes!" the boy next to Cassie said. "We should make her play with her skate laces tied together to give us a chance."

"Nah! We'll do okay," Cassie said. "If we could get Arlo to come out, the teachers wouldn't stand a chance!"

"Quit being so pushy!" I snapped at her. "All you ever talk about is hockey, hockey, hockey! It just makes me sick! Why don't you just bug off? I've got more exciting things to do." Then I buried my head between my knees so I wouldn't have to look at anybody.

The assembly started a few seconds later. We watched a bunch of Hawaiian hula dancers perform some traditional dances. Afterward, Mr. Butterworth stood at the front of the gym and announced, "Time once again for our Perfect Attendance draw, boys and girls! The names of all the kids with perfect attendance over the past month are in this bucket. I'll be drawing out one name for this month's prize—a brand-new hockey stick!"

Surprise! Surprise! What else would the prize be at this hockey-crazy school?

"And this month's winner is…" Mr. Butterworth said, rummaging around in the bucket and pulling out a slip of paper, "Arlo Billingsly!"

What? Me? Perfect attendance? This was only my second day. There must be some mistake! But no one seemed to think so. Everyone clapped and cheered. I staggered up to the front of the assembly feeling really stunned.

"Congratulations, Arlo!" Mr. Butterworth said. "We're all looking forward to seeing you make use of this hockey stick!" There was more clapping and cheering.

I think the word is "conspiracy." There seemed to be a conspiracy to get me out on the ice so I could make a complete fool of myself!

But they could try as hard as they wanted. They couldn't force me! Instead of playing hockey against the teachers, I'd be with my real friends in the Dumpster.

CHAPTER 8

After lunch, everyone was yammering about the hockey game between the teachers and the students. That's all they could think about.

"Did you see the save Mrs. Pendergast made?"

"Yeah! It was the greatest save ever made by a kindergarten teacher!"

"I'll say! I never knew she could do the splits like that."

"I don't think she did, either."

They talked about Bob Wilson's shot from the blue line that deflected off Mr. Butterworth's rear end and into his own net. They talked about Mr. Ludlow, the janitor, who had a breakaway but ended up tripping on the blue line and falling flat on his face. They talked about all the chances they should have scored on and the fluky plays by the teachers. And they talked about Mrs. Pendergast's save that gave the teachers their 6–5 win.

Everyone had an extra ten minutes to talk about the game because Mrs. Armstrong was late coming back to class. When she finally came into the room, we could see why she was late. She was holding an ice pack over her right eye.

She stood at the front of the room and took the ice pack off so we could see her giant shiner. But she was still smiling. "Great game, eh?" she said. The kids all grumbled. "And Cassie Galloway, the next time you high-stick me, you'll get an F in PE!" Mrs. Armstrong laughed. The rest of the class joined in. But I didn't. I was too busy looking up at the clock. It said 1:10. In five minutes I had a meeting in the boys' washroom.

"We've got some work to catch up on," Mrs. Armstrong announced. "Get your science books out and work on your geology projects. I'll be coming around to help out if you have any problems."

I looked at the clock again: 1:11. I should give myself about a minute to get from the class to the washroom. At 1:14 I would raise my hand and ask to go to the washroom.

I stared at the second hand on the clock. It seemed to move in slow motion to 1:12.

"Arlo, you've got work to do!" Mrs. Armstrong said from across the room. I thought I'd better look like I was doing something. Hmm. Geology. We never did that at my old school. Rocks weren't important to Mrs. Peachly. She was into magnetism. For science, she always dusted off an old set of magnets and we'd try to figure out what surfaces the magnets would stick to. I got in trouble when I told the whole class that my magnet had stuck to Sarah Steele's head.

At 1:13, Mrs. Armstrong was across the room, bent over a desk, helping some kid with his geology project. I didn't find these rocks very interesting. They didn't explode, and you couldn't eat them or teach them to do tricks. They just sat there—like rocks. Mrs. Armstrong seemed pretty interested in them, though.

1:14. Now my heart was beating really hard. Only a minute until I was supposed to be in the washroom. I put my hand up, but Mrs. Armstrong had her back to me. I had to find a way to get her attention.

I cleared my throat. She didn't move. I cleared my throat again, more loudly. Twice more.

Mrs. Armstrong turned around and looked at me. "I'll be there in a few minutes, Arlo. Just be patient."

A few minutes! I didn't have a few minutes! Already the hands on the clock looked like they were speeding up and closing in on 1:15.

I put my hand up again and snapped my fingers.

Finally Mrs. Armstrong looked over at me, shot me an ugly glare and said, "Arlo! I told you to be patient. Wait like the others!" Obviously, Mrs. Armstrong was not going to budge. I'd have to do something else to get her attention. Something more drastic.

I crossed my legs and held my breath until my face

turned purple. Then I started rocking back and forth, holding my stomach.

"Arlo! What is it?" I could sense some impatience in her voice, but I didn't care at this point.

"Sorry, Mrs. Armstrong, but I've got to go really badly!" I said, rocking back and forth even faster. I wanted to make it clear that unless she let me go, there would be an unpleasant accident.

"Well, you'd better go, then," she finally said, shaking her head in dismay. As I ran out of the class, I glanced up at the clock. 1:17! I hoped I wasn't too late.

I ran at full speed to the boys' washroom. Just as I got there, a little kid from kindergarten class was heading through the door. "Stop!" I called. "You can't go in there!"

"Why not?" the kid asked.

"Well, because...because a strange new species of water snake that lives in the sewers was seen swimming in one of the toilets. Mr. Butterworth wants everyone to stay out until they can get a...a...snake charmer to come in and charm the snake out of the toilet!"

"Really?" the little kid gasped.

"Oh yeah!" I said. "Some kid was using the toilet and got bitten by a snake on the you-know-where."

"He got bitten on the you-know-where?" he said. Amazing! It looked like this kid believed every word I said.

"Yep. And you don't want to get bitten on the you-know-where, so you better not go in the you-know-there!" The kid bolted back to his class. I figured he'd probably wait until he got home to go to the bathroom.

I pushed the door to the washroom open and ran in. I couldn't see anyone. Was I too late? Had the guys already given up on me? The door swung shut behind me, and there stood Rocko and Pinball.

"Sorry I'm late, but Mrs. Arm—"

"Shh!" Pinball said, holding his index finger over his lips.

"But where's X?" I asked.

"Hey! You shut up or you'll miss your chance," Pinball whispered in a voice that was quiet but angry.

"But before I do this, at least can't you guys tell me who X is?" I said.

"Listen up! There are some questions even we don't ask. All we know is X is watching. You better believe it. He knows every step you take. That's all you have to know," Pinball went on. "X gave us all the details. First we have to take care of the janitor."

Take care of the janitor? What did they mean by that? Tie him up and gag him? Knock him unconscious with a rubber chicken? Lock him in the teachers' washroom? They didn't explain. They seemed to know what they were doing, so I just followed along.

Pinball peeked out the washroom door. The hall was clear, so he waved us on, and we all made a run for it down the hall. We stopped at a door marked *Mr. J. Ludlow, Custodian.*

"This is where you get in the air ducts—through the ceiling of the janitor's room," Pinball said. "But first, let's take care of Ludlow." He unfolded a piece of paper and held it up for me to read. It said:

> *Mr. Ludlow,*
> *Please come to Room 6 immediately. There is an emergency. Bring a ladder and a bunch of tools.*
> *Miss Crumbly*

"This ought to keep Ludlow busy for a while," Pinball said, refolding the note. Rocko stayed pretty quiet. I think he was so scared he couldn't talk. All he did was keep looking over his shoulder back down the hall, watching for signs of trouble.

Pinball slid the note under Mr. Ludlow's door, and the three of us hid around the corner. Within fifteen seconds, Mr. Ludlow's door flew open, and he came charging out carrying buckets, wrenches, a mop, a broom, a toolbox and a huge stepladder. He was down the hall and out of sight in a flash.

Pinball gave the signal, and we slipped into the custodian's room, closing the door behind us.

"So, what am I supposed to do exactly?" I asked.

Pinball unrolled a crumpled wad of paper. "See this map here? X drew it especially for you." There were a bunch of squares and lines drawn on the paper. "It's a map of the air ducts in the school. We're right here, see?"

"How does X know where all the air ducts in the school go?" I asked.

"'Cause he's X, that's why!" Pinball said. "Now quit asking stupid questions and listen up."

The air ducts on the map were drawn in red. They went all over the school like streets in a city. It looked complicated. I was never any good at reading maps in the first place, but reading this one was a matter of life or death, so I paid close attention.

"You have to crawl through the air ducts from here— that's where we are now," Pinball said, pointing to a large circle on the map, "and come out here." He ran his finger across the paper and pointed to a square on the map marked *Storage Room*.

It looked like an awfully long way to me. And besides, I wasn't too crazy about crawling through those air ducts. There were a whole bunch of places where three or four ducts met, just like at an intersection, only there were no street signs. If I went down the wrong duct, I'd get lost. How would I get out of the ducts if I was lost? I could feel myself starting to panic: gurgly stomach, itchy ears, shaking knees.

"Rocko, get the vent ready," Pinball said. Rocko pulled a stepladder out from behind the door and climbed up to the vent in the ceiling. He gave the vent a huge tug, but it didn't budge.

"Hey, Pinball! Gimme a hand here!" With Rocko holding on to the vent for dear life, Pinball grabbed his knees, and the two began to swing back and forth. After a few hard swings, the vent popped loose from the ceiling in a cloud of dust and broken plaster. As Pinball and Rocko tumbled down, they knocked loose a whole shelf of janitor supplies. At least a hundred cans, boxes and bottles all came crashing down in a gigantic avalanche.

All the noise and mess made Rocko and Pinball panic. "Hurry up! Before someone comes!" Pinball whispered.

"But...but...what about...what if..." I stuttered. I was freaking out big-time.

"Shut up! There's no time! Gotta hurry!" Pinball gasped as he pressed the map into my hand and shoved me up the ladder and into the opening in the ceiling.

I slid on my belly into the air duct. It was just as X had described—a big tin tunnel with flat sides. Fortunately, it was bigger than I had imagined, and I was able to crawl on all fours without hitting my head.

I looked ahead down the air duct in the direction I was supposed to crawl. Beyond about two meters, it was pitch-black. As I started to unfold the map, I realized it would be impossible to read X's map up here. "Hey, wait a minute!" I called down through the opening in the ceiling. "It's dark in here! How am I supposed to read the map?"

"Use this," Pinball said, tossing me a flashlight. "Ludlow won't mind if you borrow it for a while. Now, get going before he comes back!"

Again I looked ahead into the darkness of the air duct. It was a great big black hole. Doubt, panic, fear...all those bad feelings suddenly hit me in the face like a cream pie. Then I thought, Maybe I'm not the first kid to try this. Maybe the last kid to try this never made it out. Maybe I'll stumble on his skeleton somewhere. Maybe hockey wasn't so bad after all!

But there was no turning back now. Rocko was pushing the vent cover back into place. Only a few streaks of light shone through the vent. The rest of the way was black. I was sealed in the air duct.

Below me I could hear Pinball and Rocko saying, "Let's get outta here! Quick!" followed by stumbling and shuffling.

"Hey, you guys!" I called. "I don't want to do this. It's creepy in here! How about giving me something else to do for the test? Rocko! Pinball! Are you guys still there?"

The only sound I heard was the thud of the janitor's room door closing.

I was on my own.

ChAPTER 9

I couldn't afford to freak out. There was no turning back, so the only thing I could do was try to stay calm, look at the map and follow the shortest route through the air ducts to the storage room.

After I switched on the flashlight, I unfolded the map and began to search for the best route to the storage room. The custodian's room was at one end of the school and the storage room was at the other end. In between was a network of air ducts going in all different directions to every corner of the school. I was in a giant metal maze.

As I sat looking at the map and deciding on the best route to take, I heard a click from somewhere down the air duct and felt a huge *whoosh* of warm air. The rushing wind snatched the map out of my hands and sent it sailing out of sight into the darkness ahead of me.

"No!" I gasped. "Come back!"

Great. Here I was, stuck in a jungle of duct work

without a map. All I could do now was crawl along and hope I was lucky enough to be going in the right direction.

Crawling slowly along the duct, I felt my way through the darkness. Every so often, I'd stop and wave my hand in front of me, just to make sure I didn't crawl straight into a bend in the duct.

I wasn't sure how long I'd been crawling when I finally caught sight of a glimmer of light up ahead. When I reached the light, I discovered another vent and peered down to the room below. It was a classroom.

"Byron and Waldo! Where in the world have you two been?" the teacher said.

"Um...well...we were sharpening our pencils." I recognized that voice. It was Pinball! I wondered if he was Byron or Waldo.

"Yeah, he's right. We love to sharpen our pencils in the janitor's room." That was Rocko. No doubt about that.

"You left the room to sharpen your pencils? What's wrong with our classroom's pencil sharpener?" the teacher demanded.

"Well...ah...it's too loud. Yeah, it's too loud."

"Too loud?" the teacher said.

"Yeah. We don't like disturbing all the hard-working students in this class by grinding that loud pencil sharpener," Pinball said.

"He's right. I hate hearing the pencil sharpener when I'm using my brain for thinking," Rocko added.

"That's one of the most ridiculous excuses I've ever heard in my entire thirty-five years of teaching!" the teacher shouted.

After hearing their lame excuse for disappearing from their class, I knew I'd have to come up with something more believable when I finally got back to my classroom. If I ever got back, that is!

I crawled past the vent and continued on my way through the air duct. A few minutes later, I reached a place where the air duct split in two. This was where the map would have come in handy, but all I could do now was guess which was the right way to go. "Eenie, meenie…" I started, and when I'd finished, I was pointing left.

A little more crawling. Yikes! Another intersection with air ducts going three directions this time. I decided to go to my right. I had a hunch it was the right direction.

When I reached the next vent, I heard a familiar voice. So much for my hunches. It was Mrs. Armstrong. This was great! I could spy on my own class.

"Has anyone seen Arlo?" Mrs. Armstrong asked. I gulped. I almost replied, "I'm here!" but I didn't know what Mrs. Armstrong would think or do if she heard my voice coming from an air vent in the ceiling.

"Nope. He's not here," Elsa said. "He said he was going to the washroom, but that was ages ago. He must be up to something."

"Maybe he got lost," Cassie said.

"Yes, maybe he took a wrong turn somewhere.

Spatial orientation in this school can be rather confusing to the uninitiated," a squeaky voice said. I couldn't see the speaker, but I knew it was that weird kid, Cedric. "I shall go and seek his whereabouts if that would please you, Mrs. Armstrong."

"Thank you, Cedric," Mrs. Armstrong replied.

Cedric might come looking for me, but I was pretty sure he'd never find me.

I continued to crawl, hoping that my classroom was on the way to the storage room.

It didn't take long to reach the next vent. Peering down into the classroom, I could see two adults talking.

"I'm sure the note said there was an emergency in this room, Miss Crumbly." It was the janitor, Mr. Ludlow.

"Well, there's certainly no emergency in here. At least, there wasn't until you broke the window with that ladder of yours," said a woman's voice.

"But...the note...it was even signed by you!"

"Mr. Ludlow, you must have the wrong Miss Crumbly, because I certainly didn't sign any note about an emergency in my classroom. Can you show me the note?"

"No, I didn't bring it with me. I'll go back and check my supply room. It's got to be there."

One thing I did remember from my quick look at X's map of the school was that Miss Crumbly's class was in the opposite direction from the storage room. I had gone in completely the wrong direction. There was nothing I could do but crawl on.

I passed over a ukulele class. I think they were trying to play "When the Saints Go Marching In," but it sounded more like a train accident in progress.

Then I passed over what looked like the Learning Assistance room. A teacher was working with a small group of kids. "Remember, the rule is *i* before *e* except after *c*. Take the word 'ceiling,' for example." The teacher paused as everyone looked up in my direction.

I kept crawling.

In another classroom, a teacher called out, "Samantha! Are you passing notes in class again?"

"No, Mr. Mandible. This piece of paper…it just fell out of that vent in the ceiling. It looks like a treasure map or something."

"Let me see it," the teacher said.

I kept crawling. Faster this time.

The next room I reached was the boys' washroom. The door swung open and two little kids walked in. I started to crawl on my way, but something terrible happened: It was awfully dusty in the ducts, and I sneezed.

"What was that!" one little kid said.

"I dunno!" said the other.

"It sounded like it came from up in the ceiling! We'd better go tell Mr. Butterworth!"

They turned to leave. I knew I had to do something—right away. The last thing I wanted was for Mr. Butterworth to get suspicious about strange things happening up in the air ducts.

Using my deepest, gruffest voice, I yelled, "STOP!"
It helped that my voice echoed a little in the metal duct.
"DO NOT GO ANY FARTHER, LITTLE BOYS! I AM
THE BEAST THAT LIVES IN THE CEILING! I CAN
GO ANYWHERE IN THE SCHOOL AND NO ONE
CAN STOP ME! I EAT DUST AND DEAD MICE, BUT
IF YOU TELL MR. BUTTERWORTH ABOUT ME,
I WILL EAT YOU UP!"

"Yikes!" the two boys screamed as they ran out the
door, probably running faster than they'd ever run in their
lives. I heard their footsteps pounding down the hall at
high speed, soon followed by the thundering voice of
Mr. Butterworth.

"Hey, you kids! Slow down! Why are you in such a
hurry?"

"It's...it's...it's...," one boy stammered, but nothing
else came out.

"It's nothing," said the other boy.

"Why do you keep looking up at the ceiling?" Mr.
Butterworth asked.

"No reason," said the first boy.

"He's right," said the second one. "We didn't hear
anything in the ceiling, did we, Jason?"

"EXCEPT A MONSTER! THERE'S A MONSTER
UP IN THE CEILING OF THE WASHROOM!" the
first kid yelled. "AND HE SAID HE'S GOING TO EAT
US UP!"

"A monster? In the ceiling?" Mr. Butterworth laughed.

"Don't you worry, boys. I can assure you there's nothing up in that ceiling to worry about."

I crawled as fast as my hands and knees could carry me. The farther I could get away from the washroom, the better. I turned left, then right, then left again until I lost track of how many turns I'd taken. After about six or seven more turns, I was completely lost.

Then I heard a familiar voice. It was Mrs. Armstrong again.

"Cedric? Any sign of Arlo?" she asked.

"No sign at all, Mrs. Armstrong. However, there were two small children coming down the hall at a rather high speed, using very loud voices to describe a monster in the ceiling."

"Such wild imaginations," Mrs. Armstrong chuckled.

"Quite the contrary, Mrs. Armstrong. I feel their minds are polluted with the drivel of excessive pop culture consumption through movies, television and video games, leading to such delusions," Cedric said.

"Whatever you say, Cedric," Mrs. Armstrong said.

The good news was that Cedric had taken Mrs. Armstrong's mind off my disappearance. The bad news was that after all my crawling around, I was back at my own classroom. I was going in circles. Maybe I would spend the rest of my life up in the ceiling of the school after all!

I continued on my way, trying to crawl as quickly as possible, thumping along on my hands and knees. As I passed over one classroom, the teacher said, "That's funny. Thunder in February. How unusual." After that I tried to slide my knees and hands a little more quietly along the metal duct.

More air vents, more classrooms, but no storage room. I hadn't crawled this much since I was a one-year-old, and my knees were killing me. Not only that, I was dripping with sweat from the blasts of warm air that swept through the ducts whenever the furnace came on. Stopping for a rest, I peered down through a vent to see a desk stacked high with papers. Against the wall beside the desk were shelves filled with books like *The Principal's Cookbook* and *Bedtime Stories for Principals*. It didn't take a rocket scientist to figure out that I was above the principal's office.

"I'm really concerned about him, Mr. Butterworth." Mrs. Armstrong's voice came from just outside the office door. "He disappeared a while back, and I haven't seen a sign of him since. I hope he's not lost."

"That's strange," Mr. Butterworth said. "I was out in the hall and didn't see hide nor hair of him. There were just two kids going on about some monster in the ceiling. Let's do one more thorough search of the school, and if we can't find him, we'll call his mother. Maybe he was upset about something and ran home. Starting at a new school can be pretty stressful." I heard the door to the office close as they left.

I knew I had to find the storage room and get back to class before Mrs. Armstrong and Mr. Butterworth finished their search of the school. Otherwise, if I was still rattling around in the air ducts and they couldn't find me, they'd phone my mother, who would panic and call 9-1-1. The police would tear around town with their sirens screaming, looking for me, but I'd really still be at school. Then, if I did show up, everyone, including the principal, my teacher, Mom and the police, would want to know where I'd been. And when I told them I was crawling around in the air ducts, I'd probably be washing police cars for the rest of my childhood.

And even worse, if I didn't find the storage room and finish the stunt, X would never let me become a Dumpster Dude. I wouldn't be able to hang out with them, and I'd have to put up with kids bugging me about playing hockey.

All in all, it looked like I didn't have much time before major trouble would erupt. I crawled across the vent at top speed, determined to find the storage room before Mr. Butterworth and Mrs. Armstrong finished their search of the school.

As I launched myself through the air duct, the pounding of my knees jarred loose the vent in the ceiling of the principal's office. My stomach shot up into my throat as I felt the metal vent give way. I did a free fall through the hole in the ceiling, clutching the broken vent for dear life, and landed right in the middle of Mr. Butterworth's desk.

CHAPTER 10

G ood thing Mr. Butterworth had a messy desk; a stack of papers cushioned my fall. I rolled off his desk onto the floor, still holding the broken air vent. As I dusted off the bits of plaster and dust balls that had fallen along with me, I glanced around and saw the office was empty. No one had seen me.

As I started looking for a way to climb back into the ceiling, I heard footsteps in the hall heading my way. If I was caught in the principal's office with no principal and a broken air vent, I'd have some explaining to do. With no time to climb back into the ceiling, I decided to head out the door—and fast!

The footsteps in the hall belonged to Mr. Ludlow, the custodian. He was carrying his ladder and a load of tools, mumbling to himself, "I was sure that note said Miss Crumbly's room. I was sure of it. Must have left it in my room…"

Mr. Ludlow was headed back to the custodian's room, and I knew when he found that gigantic mess Pinball and Rocko had made, he'd sound the alarm. "Excuse me, Mr. Ludlow!" I called. "There's a problem in Mr. Butterworth's office. Something to do with an air vent or something."

"Are you sure?" He eyed me suspiciously. "I just went down to Miss Crumbly's room for some emergency, and there was no problem. No problem, that is, until I broke the window with this darn-tootin' ladder."

"This is an emergency for sure. I saw the vent with my very own eyes. It looks pretty serious," I said, looking like I meant every word.

"It does? Well, I guess I'd better head on down while I have my ladder and check it out," Mr. Ludlow said, turning toward Mr. Butterworth's office. There were no windows around for him to break, but something else got in the way of his ladder. As he swung that long ladder around, one end smacked into the fire alarm. In the wink of an eye, bells were blaring all over the school. Moments later, kids started streaming out of the building into the freezing cold.

"There's no time to grab your jackets! Just go straight outside!" teachers ordered. "No, I don't care if you only have socks on your feet! Move it!" A class ran out of the gym, wearing only shorts and T-shirts.

At the end of the hall, the last few kids from my own class were filing out the door. I ran down the hall and joined the back of the line. Mr. Butterworth passed me going the other way, but he didn't see me. He was too busy sniffing for smoke.

Outside, Mrs. Armstrong did a roll call. When she finally came to the end of the list, she called, "And Arlo! Where in the world is Arlo?"

"Present!" I answered.

She looked up, and her jaw dropped, her mouth opened wide and her eyeballs looked like they were ready to pop out of their sockets. "Arlo! Where have you been?"

"Oh…well…I've…I've…been sharpening my pencil in the library. I find the pencil sharpener in our class is too loud…"

It was 3:10 PM. I was standing out in front of the school, waiting for Mom to pick me up. A couple of little kids beside me were talking while they waited for their bus.

"Was it the same kid who rode his bike through the assembly?"

"Probably."

"How did he get into the ceiling?"

"I heard he cut a hole in the ceiling with a pocketknife and climbed in. Then he crawled around and ended up in Mr. Butterworth's office."

"Wow! The principal's office!"

"Yeah! Then he cut another hole and climbed down

onto the desk just as Mr. Butterworth walked in."

"Yikes! Did he get away?"

"Get away? Are you kidding? The kid knows karate, so he chopped Mr. Butterworth's desk in two with his bare hand..."

"With his bare hand!"

"And then he climbed the bookshelves and went back up through the hole in the ceiling."

"You're kidding! And then where'd he go?"

"No one knows. Some people think he might still be up there somewhere in the ceiling."

When Mom finally arrived, I was glad to see she had gotten her own car running. The kids at the bus stop wouldn't be able to bug me about the manure-mobile any more.

As I slid into the passenger seat, Mom said with a hopeful grin, "So, was your second day any better than your first?"

"Well..." I rolled my eyes and scrunched my face, looking thoughtful. "It was okay. Kind of boring, actually."

"Oh, well. After your first day, you should probably be happy with boring. It just means you're getting used to things around here." She smiled. Mom seemed to be look-ing for any possible speck of goodness in my reactions.

"I still think the school's a converted pig barn, and the

kids are all weird, and the teachers aren't nearly as good as the ones in Victoria," I added, just to make sure she didn't think I was giving in. "I still think we should move back."

Mom sighed again, just like she had yesterday. "It'll take time, Arlo. You've got a lot of adjustments to make, and adjustments take time."

As Mom started pulling the car out of the parking lot, Mr. Butterworth came running over. Leaning on Mom's window, he called across to me, "So, how did your second day go, Arlo? Getting to know your way around the school a bit better?"

I nodded.

"I hope your day was better than mine. It was crazy around here today! I had little kids saying there were monsters in the ceiling, a broken window in the grade two room, a false fire alarm, another kid reporting snakes in the toilets, the air vent in my office fell down and a shelf in the custodian's room gave way—all within about half an hour!"

"Wow!" Mom said. "Sounds like some funny stuff going on. You'd better watch that new student of yours," she joked, putting her hand on top of my head and messing up my hair. "I'm sure he had something to do with it!"

Mom laughed. Mr. Butterworth laughed. But I didn't.

Mom was making dinner while I was trying to watch TV. The picture was so snowy, I wasn't sure whether I was watching half-pipe snowboarding, pro wrestling or ballet dancing. The other channel only became clear enough to watch if I grabbed the coat-hanger antenna on the back of the TV with my left hand, stood up on a chair and held my right hand over my head. This wasn't the most comfortable position for relaxing in front of the TV after a tough day at school.

Back in Victoria, the people who lived above us let me come up and watch their TV any time I wanted. They got at least seven thousand channels.

I yelled to Mom in the kitchen, "Even if everything in East Bend was great—which it isn't—the lousy TV reception is reason enough for us to move back to Victoria as far as I'm concerned."

But of course, when I said this, Mom replied, "You watched too much TV in Victoria anyway, Arlo. This way you'll be forced to entertain yourself with activities that are better for you, like reading."

"Mom, get real for a minute," I yelled back. "I read all day in school, so I'm not about to read in my spare time. That would be like you coming home after work and bandaging people up or giving them shots just for the fun of it."

"Well, you could go outside," she suggested. "Get some fresh air and exercise."

"Fresh air? I'll say it's fresh air. May I remind you that

the air outside is so 'fresh' it freezes exposed skin in under a minute! If I take a deep breath, my lungs will freeze solid and I'll have to wait until spring to breathe again!"

Mom sighed. I think she was getting tired of arguing. Maybe I was finally starting to wear her down. I had a feeling that moving back to Victoria was just around the corner.

I'd given up on the snowboarding/wrestling/ballet channel and was climbing up on a chair with my left hand on the coat hanger when the phone rang. It was the first call we'd had since we'd moved here. Probably Grandpa and Grandma calling from Arizona to see how we were doing. I could hardly wait to get hold of that phone and tell them how things really were. They'd probably drive straight up here in their motor home and rescue me from this horrible place.

Mom answered. "Hello?...Yes, it is...Oh, hello, Mrs. Smiley."

Mrs. Smiley? Who in the world was Mrs. Smiley?

"Yes...yes...yes, it was nice meeting you today too...yes...yes...uh-huh...ooh, that sounds like fun. I'll let you talk to him."

Mom held the phone out to me. "It's Mrs. Smiley. Her son Nate's in your class. You're being invited to his birthday party. Nate wants to talk to you."

I took the phone as Mom headed back to the kitchen. "Hello?" I said.

"Hi, Arlo? This is Nate...Nate Smiley...I sit right in front of Elsa."

"Oh yeah. Right. Hi," I replied, sounding as unfriendly as possible. Nate was a geek. At least, that's what Pinball had told me. His parents owned the grocery store. Pinball said Nate was a spoiled brat.

"Um, well, I'm having a birthday party this Friday night, and we were wondering if you wanted to come. Every year my dad rents the arena in town at midnight, and we have a hockey game that goes all night. We call it Midnight Madness. Can you make it?"

I couldn't believe it. They didn't even have normal birthday parties around here! Hadn't they heard of bowling? At least you don't have to wear skates for that. And what's the big thrill about playing hockey at midnight, anyway? It's nothing compared to crawling around the school in the air ducts!

"Oh...Hmm...Next Friday, you say? That's too bad, because...because...well, my uncle from...from...Iceland will be visiting, and he promised to...to...to give me accordion lessons when he's here, so I'll be too busy Friday night practicing the accordion with my Uncle Wilf from Iceland."

After I hung up, Mom returned from the kitchen. She obviously hadn't heard what I'd said. "That was nice of Nate to invite you," she said. "It sounds like it could be a lot of fun. And you'll finally get a chance to try out your new skates and hockey stick!"

I didn't tell Mom I wasn't going to the party. I'd tell her later, when I could think up a good excuse. Today my brain had made up all the excuses it could think of. I went back to watching the snowboarding/wrestling/ballet channel.

CHAPTER 11

The next morning, I couldn't wait to get to the Dumpster at recess. I was trying my best to concentrate on math, but it was tough. I kept thinking about X declaring me a lifetime member of the Dumpster Dudes, presenting me with my membership card and telling me all about the secret handshake. Even though I hadn't exactly reached the storage room yesterday, I'd come pretty close. Close enough to become a member.

"*Psst*!" It was Johnny Steinbach, poking me in the back, waking me up from my daydream. Mrs. Armstrong was droning on about double-digit multiplication.

"Hey, Arlo," Johnny whispered. "You know why the fire alarm went off yesterday?"

I shook my head.

"Some kid got sucked up through a heating vent," he said. "He was washing his hands in the washroom and *swoosh*! The air lifted him right off the ground and up through the vent. I heard they had to call the fire department to get him out. If you ask me, I'm never going to the washroom here again! What d'you think?"

I shrugged my shoulders and pretended to be working on my math, but inside I was glowing with pride. Everyone was still talking about yesterday. But no one knew the truth. That's how legends were made.

Looking at the clock, I saw that recess was in ten minutes, and I would be attending my first meeting as a lifetime member of the legendary Dumpster Dudes!

When the bell finally went, Mrs. Armstrong kept me behind for a few extra minutes because I couldn't get double-digit multiplication. I didn't care. I wouldn't need double-digit multiplication now that I was a Dumpster Dude. We were lifetime members, so we'd still be doing wild and crazy stuff when we were adults. We'd become professional Dumpster Dudes and get paid millions of dollars to do crazy stunts. It would be great!

By the time I climbed into the Dumpster, Pinball and Rocko were already there.

"Hey! There's the man!" Pinball said, slapping me on the back. "You are one crazy dude!"

"Yeah, I'll say!" Rocko said. "Landing in the principal's office! That's even better than what X told you to do!"

The light clicked on, and I heard X's voice. "Enough!" He didn't sound pleased.

"How'd I do, X?" I asked.

"Not *too* bad," he said very slowly. I didn't like the

way he emphasized the *too*. I had a feeling. A bad feeling.

"So I...I...I did what you said. I went through the air ducts all the way from..."

"The principal's office is not the storage room, in case you didn't know!" X growled.

"But, hey, X, isn't the principal's office even better than some dumb storage room?" Pinball said.

"Yeah," Rocko added. "A storage room's just full of books and paper and stuff. But the principal's office is full of principal!"

"Silence, you buffoons! I'll be the judge of success and failure. The two of you don't have a clue."

"Sorry, X," Pinball mumbled.

"Yeah. Sorry, X," Rocko said.

"The instructions were to crawl from the janitor's room to the storage room," X said, his voice a little louder this time.

"I know, I know," I said. "But, hey! Shouldn't landing in the principal's office count for something? I mean, I might have landed right in Mr. Butterworth's lap! That should be worth something! Shouldn't it, X?"

There was a long silent pause. Maybe X hadn't made up his mind. Or maybe he was just letting me stew and fuss.

Finally he spoke. "Landing in the principal's office was good. Yes, it was good. But to pass the test and become one of us, you must do EXACTLY as I say."

"Yeah," I pleaded, "but I think the principal's office is more..."

X cleared his throat, and I knew it was time to shut my mouth. I was acting just like Rocko and Pinball.

"EXACTLY as I say," X repeated. I began to wonder if his name stood for "eXactly."

"You were close...very close," X said. "So...instead of kicking you out, I'm giving you one more chance."

"Gee, thanks, X! I really appreciate it. I won't let you down this time," I stammered with excitement. I couldn't stand the thought of being kicked out of the club, so when X decided to give me another chance, I felt a great rush of relief. "Do you want me to go through the air ducts again?"

There was a really long pause. X didn't make a sound. Finally he said, "No, this time it will be something different."

"Sure thing, X," I said. "Whatever you say, X!"

"I wouldn't say that!" Pinball chuckled. "Wait'll you hear what you've gotta do, first!"

"Yeah!" Rocko snorted. "X'll probably make it something really bad!"

"There is no such thing as a bad stunt," X said, speaking more loudly than normal. "It's just that some stunts are more wild and crazy than others."

"Yeah. That's what I meant," Rocko said.

"So, what's the stunt? What do I have to do for my test, huh?" I asked. I couldn't wait any longer. I had to know what I'd be doing. I figured it couldn't be any worse than climbing around the school through those smelly old air ducts.

"For your next test, you'll need a bike," X said. "Have you got one?"

Before I could answer X's question, we heard voices outside the Dumpster. Adult voices. One sounded like Mr. Ludlow. The other sounded like the grade seven teacher, Mr. Crow.

"How did the fish dissections go?" Mr. Ludlow asked.

"Pretty good. Only two kids threw up, so it wasn't too bad," Mr. Crow answered.

"I don't blame them. All that blood and fish guts—the smell's awful! Your class was stinking up the whole school!"

"Oh, well," Mr. Crow said. "Once they're in the Dumpster, we can air the school out."

As the lid creaked open, we squeezed to the far corners, hoping Crow and Ludlow wouldn't see us. But we didn't see Crow's or Ludlow's face poking over the side of the Dumpster. All we saw were two huge garbage bags tossed into the Dumpster, where they landed with a strange squishy sound. The bags split open, and two streams of slimy, bloody, stinky fish guts slithered out across the inside of the Dumpster. The lid slammed shut. No one said anything for a while, as we waited for Crow and Ludlow to walk away from the Dumpster.

After what seemed like a very long period of silence, Rocko said, "Maybe we should think about finding another place for our meetings, huh, X?"

There I was. Skates on my feet, a hockey stick in my hand. Mom couldn't find a real helmet, so she made me wear a cooking pot on my head. The only other padding I had was a pillow stuffed down the back of my pants. I didn't have gloves, so Mom gave me oven mitts shaped like fish.

Kids were *whooshing* all around me. I didn't recognize any of them. They were just blurs as they flew past, showering me with sprays of snow from their skate blades.

But I couldn't move my feet. It was like they were frozen into the ice. Then someone zoomed past and hooked my skate with the blade of their stick. My skates suddenly flipped up into the air, and I went smashing onto the ice. I tried to get up, but my skates just slid around. Then I noticed my skate blades had changed into banana peels.

I felt a thud. The puck had hit me. But it didn't bounce away. It went down the back of my pants. Suddenly I was surrounded by kids swatting at the puck, which was still in the seat of my pants. I slid all over the ice like a giant human puck.

One kid took a great big slap shot and I flew toward the net. Mrs. Pendergast, the kindergarten teacher, was in goal. She deflected me wide of the net, with her stick glancing off my right ear. I went crashing into the end boards.

That's when I woke up.

This was bad. Really bad. Now I was even dreaming about that stupid game.

In class the next morning, my mind was not on whatever Mrs. Armstrong was doing at the front of the classroom. I was thinking about X's plans for my second test. After the arrival of the fish guts in the Dumpster, he hadn't given me any more details other than the need for a bike. I just hoped it wouldn't have anything to do with school assemblies.

"Are there any school assemblies planned for the next while, Mrs. Armstrong?" I asked at the end of the class.

"Hmm, now let me think. Oh yes, there are. The police are bringing their dogs in for a demonstration. They do it every year. It's wonderful to see how well trained those dogs are. I guess they have to be, considering the size of their teeth and how fast they are!"

"Oh," I said. I got that funny feeling in my stomach again—the one where it feels like someone's testing a nuclear bomb in my gut. Everything churns and gurgles and threatens to explode.

I sat at my desk and wondered which would be worse—flopping around on the ice and becoming a human puck or having one of those police dogs chase me down and sink its giant fangs into my leg as I rode a bike through the assembly.

During the second class, which I think was spelling, there was a knock at the classroom door. Mrs. Armstrong opened the door and a hand reached through, giving her a note. After reading it, she looked really puzzled.

"This is funny. I've never heard of this before," she

mumbled, walking over to me. "Arlo, I've just been given a note. The school nurse wants you to come down to the medical room to have your feet inspected."

"My feet inspected?" I said, just as puzzled as Mrs. Armstrong.

"That's what the note says."

This sounded really strange. A foot inspection? It seemed like a good time to panic. "I've never had my feet inspected before! What happens if I fail? They'll probably give me a foot transplant, and I'll probably have different-sized feet and none of my shoes will fit so I'll have to…"

"Arlo, Arlo, Arlo! Don't panic. I'm sure it's nothing serious," Mrs. Armstrong said in a soothing voice.

"Does everyone in the school have their feet inspected?" I asked.

"Um…well…no," she mumbled.

"Then why do I have to have my feet inspected?"

"I don't know. But I'm sure it's nothing to worry about," she said.

"Maybe the school nurse thinks I walk funny. Maybe she thinks I've got some strange fungus growing on my feet and it'll spread and take over the whole school, and eventually everyone will walk just like me and…"

Suddenly, Cedric appeared out of nowhere, butting into our conversation. "It is probably part of the new study being conducted by the United Nations Public Health Department on the health of preadolescent feet as they compare to similar-aged feet in developing countries in the Southern Hemisphere," he squeaked. "I read something about it in the December issue of *Scientific American*. You, Arlo, are one of the lucky ones chosen for the study. Go ahead and do your part for modern science."

Mrs. Armstrong grinned and said, "Well, there you go, Arlo. You should actually be pleased to be called down for a foot inspection. It sounds like quite an honor to be a part of…of…whatever Cedric was talking about. The medical room is right beside the office," she added.

As soon as I stepped through the door into the hallway, I knew this wasn't about a United Nations study of preadolescent feet. And I knew who the school nurse was. She didn't wear a nurse's uniform, and she didn't ask me about my feet. She wasn't even a she. The "nurse" was Pinball. Without saying a word, he pointed to the back door of the school.

CHAPTER 12

I followed him outside, even though I hadn't brought my jacket. As we walked around to the back of the school, my teeth started chattering. I don't know if it was the cold or a bad case of nerves. Or both.

Pinball led me to a pile of cardboard boxes behind the Dumpster. He pulled aside some boxes and there was Rocko, holding a little BMX bike. It looked like the same one X had ridden through the assembly. They wouldn't make me ride through the police dog assembly! Or would they? No one was that stupid. Not even me.

"This is what X wants you to do," Pinball said, pushing the bike over to me. "You ride this bike through the back door of the school, down the hall, past the office and out the front door. Then you ride across the parking lot to the back of the school and ditch the bike in the Dumpster. Got it?"

"Um…I…I…guess so. But what if Mr. B-B-Butterworth sees me?" I'd never stuttered like this before. But I'd never been this scared and cold either.

"Just ride faster. If you can't outrun Butterworth on a bike, X won't want you in the Dumpster. Now, me and Rocko gotta go."

"Yeah," Rocko chuckled. "I put some plastic vomit in the back corner of the room. I told the teacher that Pinball barfed. And the teacher believed me! So now I'm getting stuff to clean it up, and Pinball's supposed to be headed for the sick room."

"Oh, I almost forgot," Pinball said. "Wear these." He tossed me a ski mask and black sweater. They were the same ones X had worn on his ride through the assembly. "X said to wear them with honor," Pinball said as he and Rocko headed back around the school to a fire door they'd left propped open. "And remember. X said he's watching your every move. He knows EVERYTHING you do."

"Hey! Before you guys go, just tell me one thing," I called as they slipped through the door. "Why doesn't X ever come out and help get me ready for the stunts? Why does he always get you guys to do all the dirty work?"

Pinball and Rocko stopped in their tracks and turned around, staring back at me. "There are some questions no one's supposed to ask about X. And that's one of them. Just do as you're told!"

"But does X ever leave the Dumpster? Does he go to the school? If I'm going to join this club, don't you think you could at least tell…"

"There are some things even we don't know about X,"

Pinball said, with Rocko nodding in agreement. "No one does. X is just X. That's it. End of story. Now, just do what you're told!"

The fire door clicked shut, leaving me alone with the little bike, the old sweater and the ski mask. Riding through the school didn't sound as scary as crawling through the air ducts. But then, there was a side to this stunt that made it more dangerous—way more dangerous.

If I was caught, I'd be wearing the same ski mask and sweater that X had worn when he ruined the recognition assembly. Mr. Butterworth would know I was mixed up with the mystery kid they could never catch. He'd probably tie me to a chair, interrogate me and demand to know all about X. If I spilled the beans and told Mr. Butterworth all about Pinball, Rocko, X and the Dumpster, that would be the end. I'd be a traitor. They'd never let me become a Dumpster Dude. As I pulled the old sweater over my head, I realized that, this time around, failure could have serious consequences.

The sweater had holes in the elbows and a stain on the front; the ski mask smelled like wet dog. I put everything on anyway. It was cold outside and I'd rather be warm and stinky in this old sweater and ski mask than be a sweet-smelling ice cube.

Before I left my hiding place behind the Dumpster, I checked to make sure no one was in sight. Everyone was still in class, so there shouldn't be many people in the halls.

Maybe the odd kid going to the washroom, but all the teachers should be out of the way.

Edging closer to the school, I peered through the back door. The coast was clear. I wheeled the bike up to the door and took one last look down the hall. Nothing. No one. Totally vacant. My timing was perfect. It was now or never. My heart started thumping again. My hands began to shake. I pulled the door open and rolled the bike into the hall. Still no one. Slinging my leg over the seat, I put one foot up on the pedal and pushed off.

I pedaled so hard, I must have burned rubber with the back tire. The water fountain flashed by in a blur. Classroom doors whizzed past as I pedaled with everything I had.

I could see the far doors at the end of the hall already. With every turn of the pedals, my safe exit got closer and closer. All I had to do was zoom by three more classroom doors, past the office and out the front door. My lifetime membership in the Dumpster Dudes was in sight! This was easy! Almost too easy!

That's when one of the classroom doors swung open. A teacher I'd never seen before stepped out of his classroom into the middle of the hall. He must have been about five feet wide and nine feet tall. At least he looked that big as my bike zoomed toward him. Not only was the teacher gigantic, he was also carrying a glass terrarium. On the side of the terrarium was a sign: *Ant Farm*.

The huge terrarium-carrying teacher blocking the hall was just as surprised to see me as I was to see him. That's probably why he dropped the terrarium.

I felt for the brakes so I could stop and turn around, and I made a surprising discovery. This bike had no brakes. Planting my foot, I leaned right and cranked the handlebars, making a sharp turn just in time to avoid the ants, the broken glass and the very big, very angry teacher.

My sharp right-hand turn had taken me into a hallway I didn't recognize. I had no idea where it went, but I hoped that maybe there was another exit door nearby. Pedaling with every ounce of energy I had, I flew by walls covered in bulletin boards toward the only door in the hallway. This door was my only hope for escape, and I figured it just had to be a fire exit door. It wasn't. A sign above the door said *Welcome to the Library. Please Enter Quietly*.

With the giant teacher thundering down the hall after me, followed by a whole army of angry ants, I couldn't turn back. I decided to take my chances in the library.

As I spun my bike through the doorway, I tried to do exactly as the sign said—enter as quietly as possible. Even though I entered the library pretty quietly, I had a feeling the librarian didn't appreciate having a kid ride through the library on a bike being chased by a gigantic, very angry teacher. I could tell the librarian wasn't too pleased by the way she started chasing me around with a fire extinguisher.

Ducking into the non-fiction section, I zigzagged between the shelves of books. The librarian almost had me in the poetry section, but as she jumped over a shelf to tackle me, she tripped on a magazine rack and set off an avalanche of *National Geographics*. The other teacher tried to cut me off over by the computers, but he tripped on an extension cord and did a face plant.

It was weird riding a bike through a library. I'd never done it before, and I can't say I'd like to do it again. Stuff kept getting in my way, like the display of Robert Munsch books that I bumped with my front tire; it toppled over like falling dominoes. I also caught the handlebars on the tail of a gigantic papier-mâché dinosaur. The worst thing of all was when I took a sharp left and flew into the quiet reading corner. The front wheel sank into a beanbag chair, and I followed this with a somersault over the handlebars, landing in a pile of stuffed animals.

The librarian was closing in on me, leaping over a stuffed zebra, pointing the fire extinguisher at me and yelling, "Don't move or I'll shoot!" But I was too quick for her and rolled out of the way at the last minute.

"After him!" the other teacher yelled, suddenly appearing out of the non-fiction section.

There wasn't time to grab the bike, so I ran toward a door. I had no idea where it led, but I had no choice at this point. Barging through the door, I stumbled outside. Finally! The exit door I'd been looking for! But the fire extinguisher-wielding librarian and the gigantic teacher hadn't given up the chase. I sprinted around the outside of the school, losing the librarian and the teacher when they hit a patch of ice and went over like human bowling pins. I didn't slow down until I'd rounded the corner and got to the front of the school. Just before reaching the front door, I ripped off the ski mask and black sweater and stuffed them in a garbage can.

Cruising through the front door, I ducked down and tried to sneak unseen and unheard past the office and back to class. Just when I thought I was home free, I heard a voice calling from the office. "Can I help you?" It was the school secretary. She glared at me suspiciously, as she did with all kids who wandered aimlessly around the halls during class time.

"Oh! Well...yes!" I said. "I'm supposed to go to the medical room. Something about a foot inspection. Mrs. Armstrong sent me."

"That's the first I've heard about foot inspections," the secretary sighed. "But the way things are going at this school, kid, it wouldn't surprise me if they decided to do brain surgery in the medical room." Shaking her head and rolling her eyes, the secretary said, "Come right on through."

I sat down on a bed. As the secretary closed the door, there was a crashing and banging in the office.

"Mrs. Springer! Mr. Watson! What's the problem?" the secretary said, sounding just a little alarmed. "You don't look so good. And why are you carrying that fire extinguisher?"

"Where is he? Where is he?" It was the librarian's voice,

angry and out of breath. I pretended to be asleep.

"Who are you talking about?"

"That...that...that masked kid on the bike!" Mr. Watson shouted.

"I'm afraid I haven't seen anyone ride a bike through the office lately. And the only student here is that new boy, Arlo, who has something wrong with his feet."

I heard the librarian and the gigantic angry teacher stomp out of the office. Mrs. Springer was mumbling, "I'll find that kid if it's the last thing I do! He's got to be around here some...EEEK! Ants! In the hall! Ants everywhere!"

I pulled a blanket over my head. Another close call. Too close. Way too close for comfort. At least I was safe. But I wondered if X would allow me back into the Dumpster. I hadn't exactly ridden out the front door, like he told me to. But I figured riding through the library was way more dangerous. He'd have to let me in the club now. It would only be fair, after all I'd been through.

After school I waited outside for Mom. Once again, kids were talking in the bus lineup.

"Did you hear about the kid on the bike?"

"You mean the one who rode through the assembly?"

"Yeah! He did it again! This time he rode through the library."

"You're kidding!"

"No! It's true. I heard it from Marcel. He heard it from Jane. So it's got to be true!"

"Wow! The library!"

"Yeah! And he jumped right over the encyclopedia shelf on his bike!"

"Yikes!"

"Then he knocked over the magazine rack."

"Holy cow!'

"And he broke two windows when the Roald Dahl display fell over!"

"Amazing!"

"And a huge life-size papier-mâché statue of the BFG fell over and nearly crushed Mrs. Springer!"

"Did he get caught?"

"Are you kidding? Never! Mrs. Springer threw a dictionary into the spokes of his bike and he flipped over the handlebars."

"Wow! Was he hurt?"

"Are you kidding? He did a cartwheel in midair, and then he pulled Mrs. Springer's wig right off her head…"

"Mrs. Springer wears a wig?"

"Yeah! Of course! Everyone knows that. Then he took a flying leap and dove out the window above the fire escape."

"The window above the fire escape?"

"Yeah, of course."

"That's…like…that's superhuman!"

"Pretty amazing, eh?"

"Yeah!"

I knew it was me they were talking about. So what if they got a few details wrong. It didn't matter. Even though I wasn't officially a Dumpster Dude, I was already a living legend!

I wouldn't exactly say things were getting any better between Mom and me, mostly because I hadn't given up trying to convince her to move us back to Victoria.

"Do you realize the severe discipline problems Mr. Butterworth has at this school?" I told her over dinner that night. "And Mrs. Armstrong's class is even worse than the rest of the school."

"Oh?" Mom replied, looking curious.

"Yeah. Three or four fights break out during recess each day. And usually they carry over into the classroom. You don't know how hard it is to concentrate when there's a fight happening in the aisle next to your desk."

"Now, Arlo. I know you're prone to exaggeration, but that sounds just a little ridiculous," she said, shaking her head.

"No lie, Mom. I'm having a terrible time concentrating on my schoolwork because I worry that any second I might get thumped when some kid throws a punch and accidentally hits me! You don't know how hard it is to keep your handwriting neat and tidy when you're writing with one hand and pushing off a couple of kids wrestling right beside you with the other."

"Arlo Billingsly! Since when did the appearance of your handwriting ever matter to you?"

"It might not have shown up in my report cards, but Mrs. Peachly was having a very positive effect on my academic career, Mom! I was starting to feel like schoolwork was important. At my old school, I was just beginning to work and reach my potential when...well, we both know what happened. So if you really care about my education and my future, the best thing for us would be to..."

"No, Arlo! Forget it!" Mom exploded. I'd never seen her this mad. I must have finally pushed her too far. She pounded her fist on the table and raised her voice. "You might just as well forget your sneaky schemes, your little fairy tales and your ridiculous exaggerations! We are not moving back to Victoria! It's time you accepted that we are staying in our new home, our new town and your new school! You're only making it harder on yourself, not to mention me!"

I stared back, not saying a word, just blinking as my eyes filled with tears. Usually when my eyes fill with tears, Mom softens up and tries to make me feel better. But not this time. She stomped out of the kitchen into her bedroom and slammed the door. I wondered if her eyes might be filling up with tears too.

CHAPTER 13

The next morning, Mom was still angry. She didn't say much, and she wasn't her usual cheerful self. Between getting up in the morning and leaving for school, she spoke to me only three times:

"Eat your cereal."

"Brush your teeth."

"Take your lunch bag."

When she dropped me off at school, I felt a cold space between us. And it wasn't just the freezing temperature outside. I have to admit, as much as I complained and argued with Mom about this place, I hadn't realized how much I could miss her cheerful encouragement. As I left the car that morning, instead of her usual "Have a wonderful day, sweetie! I'll look forward to seeing you after school!" all she said was, "Don't slam the door!" Had Mom actually given up on me? She'd never treated me like this before. I didn't like it.

The only thing I had to look forward to was recess, when I would meet in the Dumpster with X and the guys. I could tell them all about riding through the library and my narrow escape from the librarian and the world's biggest teacher. I'd give them the gritty details of watching the terrarium crash to the floor and seeing the millions of ants scatter around the hall. I'd fill them in on my crazy rollicking ramble through the shelves in the library.

But before recess arrived, I'd have to endure two periods of classes in my dumpy classroom with all those drippy kids. Recess couldn't arrive soon enough.

First thing in the morning, Mrs. Armstrong had an announcement. "Today, as a special treat, Mr. Butterworth is going to take the class out for PE." Almost everyone in the class cheered because they knew what PE with Mr. Butterworth meant. Hockey, hockey and more hockey.

"Those of you who are unable to take part in the hockey game will have to stay in the classroom with me and work on math," our teacher added, looking right at me.

Cassie leaned toward me. "All right, Arlo! Now's your big chance to debut as a hockey star!"

"I don't think so," I mumbled.

"What? You'd rather do math than play hockey? I don't know what you've got in that skull of yours, but it sure can't be brains!"

Elsa leaned over and sneered, "I think I saw some sawdust falling out of his ears the other day."

"If you must know," I said, "I happen to be sick today. My allergies are acting up again."

"Sounds like we have another Cedric on our hands," Chuck chuckled.

"So, what are you allergic to, Arlo?" Cassie asked.

"Um…well…eggs!" I said. "I'm allergic to eggs! When I get too close to eggs, my teeth get loose and start to fall out."

"Wow. I've never heard that one before," Cassie replied, putting her finger in the gap where her front tooth used to be. "My teeth are allergic to hockey pucks, but that's never kept me from playing."

"Arlo!" Mrs. Armstrong called, motioning me to come to her desk. "I was talking to your mother on the phone last night. Mr. Butterworth, your mother, and I are concerned about you. You're not mixing with the other kids very much. It's as if you're resisting any attempts they make at friendship."

I shrugged my shoulders. I could have told her that I had friends. Three friends. And they're better friends than all the rest of the kids in the school put together. But then she'd start asking who they were and get suspicious. I knew the teachers were trying to find out who was behind all the strange things happening in the school. I wasn't going to give them any clues, so I didn't say a word. I just shrugged my shoulders.

"If you ask me, Mrs. Armstrong, Arlo doesn't have any friends because he smells like he's been hanging out in a garbage can." It was Chuck, snooping around Mrs. Armstrong's desk.

"Fortunately, Charles, no one is asking you," Mrs. Armstrong said sternly.

"Friendship is indeed a difficult relationship to achieve, especially if it is forced, hurried and artificially induced." This was, of course, Cedric. He was also snooping around Mrs. Armstrong's desk, but she didn't seem to mind. "Friendship is like a flower. You have to cultivate it in fertile soil and nurture it with tender care and plenty of sunshine. Friendship, just like gardening, takes patience." Cedric ended with a goofy cheek-to-cheek grin that lifted the glasses off his nose.

"Thank you for your words of wisdom, Cedric. You are so right." Mrs. Armstrong beamed. "This hockey game today in PE will be a good chance for you to plant those seeds! Do something with the other kids that will cultivate friendships. Your mother says that you like sports, so maybe by getting involved in hockey, you can make more friends."

I didn't say anything. No matter what I said, Mrs. Armstrong wouldn't understand. She just didn't get it. My mother didn't get it either. Neither did Mr. Butterworth or any other adults. If I'm sliding around the ice flat on my face like a human Zamboni, no one's going to like me. No one's going to want me to be part of their group. People don't want to be friends with a complete klutzomaniac.

That's why I was sticking with my real friends—X, Pinball and Rocko.

Recess finally arrived, and I bolted for the Dumpster. The others were already there; they opened the lid a crack and let me slide inside.

"So, how did I do? I must have passed, right?" I said.

"Passed?" Pinball said. "Of course you passed! No one in the history of this or probably any other school has ridden a bike through a library like that!"

"You are one crazy dude, Arlo!" Rocko said. "Tons of kids were trying to get into the library to see all the stuff you destroyed! You're like some sort of famous person, except no one knows who you are!"

The light clicked on and X's strange voice growled, "Silence! I'll be the judge of whether he passed the test or not!"

"Ah, come on, X. You've gotta admit—what Arlo did was pretty amazing," Pinball said.

"What do you know, Waldo?" X said. This was the first time I'd ever heard him use Pinball's real name. I could tell by the sound of his voice that he was sneering. "Don't ever forget why I allowed you in the Dumpster in the first place! You do remember, don't you, Waldo?"

There was a long silent pause, and then Rocko said, "I remember why he's here. His belt broke and his pants fell down right in the middle of a hockey game at recess."

"Shut your mouth, Byron! No one's asking you!" Pinball said. "At least I didn't knock my own teeth out with my very own stick!"

"How many times do I have to tell you—it was an accident!" Rocko shouted.

Wow. I thought not knowing how to skate was bad enough. But just imagine losing your pants in the middle of a game at recess. Or how about knocking out your own front teeth? I could just imagine what Chuck and Elsa and all the other kids would think of that. No wonder Pinball and Rocko hated hockey.

"Silence!" X barked. "Once again, I must remind you that you are both dimwitted klutzes! It is only my kindness that allows you into this Dumpster! So don't try to tell me if Arlo passed or failed his test!" X shone the light in my face and said, "I don't believe going into the library was part of your instructions."

"I had to go into the library, X! I had no choice! A teacher blocked the hallway, so I went a different way and the only door I saw went into the library, so I…"

"Enough!" X said. "We have given you two tests, and you have failed both of them. I'm not so sure I should give you another chance."

It felt like I was in an elevator going up and the cable had suddenly snapped. All my hopes for becoming a Dumpster Dude were falling fast. It all depended on X. He was the one who decided if I would be in the Dumpster or out in the snow with all the hockey nuts.

"I've never given a third chance before," he said finally, pausing…pausing…pausing…"So consider yourself lucky."

"Oh, I do, X! I am lucky," I agreed with enthusiasm, even though I didn't feel all that lucky. On my first two stunts, I'd been cursed with bad luck. Just when it looked like I was on my way to finishing the stunt, something went wrong. My luck was bound to change. It couldn't get any worse. It would be stupid to give up now.

"It's up to you to decide if you want to try again," X said. "You might decide not to go through with the next test."

"No, no, no!" I almost shouted. "I'll do it! I'll do it! Just tell me what it is, X! What's the next test?"

There was another long pause. The silence almost drove me crazy.

"If you have the guts…if you have what it takes to become a Dumpster Dude, you'll succeed with the next test. If you don't…if you wimp out, I don't want to see your face around here anymore. So, what's it going to be?"

"I'll do it, X! I'll do it! But tell me what I have to do!" I didn't care what he wanted me to do. I wanted to be a lifetime member more than anything. Going to the Dumpster at recess was the best part of my day. I loved how the other kids in school talked about us like we were outlaws. Sure, it was scary. Yesterday I'd broken more school rules than I could count on all my fingers and toes, but in a weird sort of way, it was the most exciting thing I'd ever done in my life. It was amazing!

But unless I succeeded in the next test, I'd be shut out of the Dumpster, and then I'd have to hang out with all the kids who had nothing on their brains but hockey.

"Please tell me, X. What do I have to do?" I pleaded.

Finally X told me. "Today at two o'clock. Your class has PE. They will be playing hockey. I am giving you a dozen eggs."

"I think I know what you want me to do," I muttered.

"Just listen," X said. "You get out of playing in the hockey game somehow and go to the equipment room in the gym. There's a ladder up to a hatch in the ceiling. Go through the hatch and up onto the roof of the gym. From up on the roof, you throw the eggs down at the game. And one of the eggs has to bean Butterworth. Get it?"

"Yeah," I said. My voice wavered. I felt excited and scared at the same time. This sounded like it could be the worst test yet. Or the best, if I pulled it off.

But what if the equipment room was locked? How would I climb a ladder carrying a dozen eggs? Sure, Mr. Butterworth was a big target, but what if I couldn't hit him with one of the eggs? And how would I get away after I'd thrown the eggs? There were a million questions whirling around my brain, but for once I kept my mouth shut. I knew X well enough by now to realize that he liked to give orders, but he hated to answer questions.

"One more thing," X said. "You're on your own with this one."

"Where will you guys be?" I asked.

"We'll be waiting right here, watching you, so we can see the whole thing with our very own eyes," X said.

Just before Pinball opened the Dumpster lid, he handed me a carton of eggs. "Good luck, Arlo," Pinball said.

"Thanks," I replied.

"He'll need more than just luck to pull this one off," X said. It sounded like he didn't think I could pass the test. But I knew I could, and I knew I would. I had to. And when I succeeded with this test, X just had to make me a lifetime member!

ChAPTER 14

The time between recess and two o'clock seemed to stretch on forever. During those four hours, I enjoyed daydreams where I imagined myself up on the roof of the gym, tossing eggs down on the ice and turning a hockey game into a wild jumble of tumbling, yolk-covered hockey players.

But I was also haunted by too many unanswered questions about pulling off this stunt. Was I being set up? Had X given me a test that I couldn't possibly pass? Maybe he hadn't even wanted me in the Dumpster in the first place.

Lost in my thoughts with all these burning questions, I snapped out of it when the booming voice of Mrs. Armstrong shouted, "It's two o'clock, everyone! Time for PE with Mr. Butterworth. And I don't have to tell you what you'll be playing."

A cheer went up from everyone in the class. Well... almost everyone. "Get your equipment and line up at the door," she ordered. Then Mrs. Armstrong added, looking right at me, "And I mean EVERYONE!" The only other kid who didn't play hockey was that little nerd Cedric. As usual, he was away at some doctor's appointment.

I noticed Mrs. Armstrong's eyebrow jump a little with surprise as I headed for the coatroom and began to put on layers of winter clothes without any complaints or excuses. Little did she know about my master plan!

I'd carefully put three eggs in each of the four pockets of my jacket. In the crowded coatroom, it was hard to slip my jacket on without bumping into anyone. Cassie accidentally knocked into me as she was picking up her stick.

"Hey! Watch it!" I shouted.

"Sorry, Arlo. How thoughtless of me," she said, rolling her eyes and shaking her head. It seemed like Cassie's annoying enthusiasm had finally come to an end. Thank goodness for that! I carefully felt in my jacket pockets— no slimy, slithery pools of broken egg. A close call.

I walked very slowly and stiffly from the coatroom to the classroom door, upright and shuffling as if I had a book resting on top of my head.

"Why are you walking so weird?" Cassie asked.

"Tender ribs," I said. "I fell out of bed last night." Again, she shook her head and rolled her eyes. I was giving her plenty of eye-rolling practice.

Finally everyone in the class was all dressed up and ready to go. "Okay, everyone! Let's..." Mrs. Armstrong paused. She was looking at me. "Arlo! Where are your skates and stick? Your mother dropped them off this morning."

"Oh, they're back in the coatroom. I can't play hockey today."

"And why not?"

"He's got bruised ribs," Cassie said. "He fell out of bed and bruised his ribs. That's why he's walking as if he's got eggs in his pockets."

"Is that correct, Arlo?" Mrs. Armstrong asked, looking sternly at me.

"No, I don't have any eggs in my pockets! Why would I have eggs in my pockets?" I said.

"I'm not asking about eggs in your pockets, Arlo. I'm asking about your bruised ribs," Mrs. Armstrong said.

"Yes, bruised ribs! Very bruised ribs! You see, I sleep in a bunk bed, and I'm not used to it. And the farmhouse we're renting is really old and the floor slopes, so I just naturally roll out of bed, and…"

"I get the picture," my teacher said, shaking her head and rolling her eyes just the way Cassie had. "If you can't play hockey during PE with Mr. Butterworth, you'll have to stay in the classroom with me and work on your math."

I knew this was coming. I knew she'd make me stay in the class while everyone else went outside. That wasn't a problem, though. All I had to do was ask if I could go to the washroom. Then I could make my way to the gym equipment room.

"Sit down, Arlo," Mrs. Armstrong ordered in a gruff voice. I'd never heard her speak like that before. She looked more stern than usual too. No big smile or sparkling eyes. Just a snarl and a frown. I didn't like the looks of it.

Mrs. Armstrong towered over me and said, "We are getting a little tired of all your excuses, Arlo. Some of the kids have gone out of their way to try to make friends with you. But all you do is avoid them! All you do is make up excuse after excuse! What is it, Arlo? Are you afraid of something? Is something bothering you?"

I shook my head. The only thing bothering me was this conversation. I was itching to get out of the classroom and up onto the roof. The eggs in my pocket were screaming, "Throw us! Throw us!"

"There's nothing you'd like to talk about? Nothing you'd like to tell me?" I could tell Mrs. Armstrong was frustrated because I wouldn't say a word.

"Well...ah...yeah, there's one thing," I said finally, breaking my silence.

"What is it?" she asked, looking hopeful.

"May I go to the washroom?"

"NO!" she boomed. Mrs. Armstrong was definitely suspicious. "The last time you went to the washroom, you were gone for nearly an hour! And while you were gone, all kinds of strange things happened! So if you are not going out to play hockey, you are going to sit right down here and do math. Now, let's take this coat off and get to work. Enough is enough!" The teacher grabbed for my jacket.

"No!" I yelled, jumping back.

"Now what's wrong?" Mrs. Armstrong demanded.

"My jacket...I mean...my ribs are tender and...I feel cold...I've got a cold coming on so I have to keep my jacket on," I stuttered. It didn't come out very well. I don't think she believed one single syllable of what I said.

"Don't be ridiculous, Arlo. You weren't wearing your jacket a few minutes ago."

"Yeah, but...but...these colds...they come on really quickly...like...like...one minute I'm fine, and the next I'm dying from a runny nose and the chills!"

"Arlo, we've had enough of your stories. Give me your jacket. Now!"

For once I couldn't think of anything to say. No original, believable excuses came flooding into my brain. All I could do was shake my head. I couldn't give her the jacket. If I did, she'd find the eggs. Mrs. Armstrong was already suspicious, but if she found the eggs, she'd know I was up to something. And she'd probably guess it was me who'd ridden the bike in the library, crawled through the air vents and caused all the trouble in the school over the past few days. That would be it. The end. I'd probably be assigned to the detention room for the next thirty years. X and the guys would never let me back in the Dumpster. I'd be the laughingstock of the whole school. Forget it! No dice! There was no chance I'd hand my jacket over to Mrs. Armstrong!

"Arlo! Give me your jacket this minute!"

I was backed into a corner with only one way out. Only one thing to do. I didn't like it, but I had no choice.

"Mrs. Armstrong? Maybe...Maybe I will play hockey after all."

She looked stunned, shaking her head as if to clear her brain. "Pardon me, Arlo. What was it that you just said?"

"I said that maybe I will play some hockey after all."

A huge smile broke out across her face. "Good for you, Arlo! That's the spirit!"

I figured she'd send me out to play, and on the way out I'd take a detour to the gym equipment room.

But I figured wrong. Once I had my skates and stick, she walked with me out to the rink, never leaving my side.

"Don't you have some marking or something to do, Mrs. Armstrong?" I asked, hoping she would leave me and go back inside. But she didn't.

"No, I think I'll stand out here and watch, Arlo. That way I can tell your mother how well you did in your first hockey game." She smiled again.

Now I was really stuck.

CHAPTER 15

"Hey, Mr. Butterworth!" Mrs. Armstrong called across the ice. "You have a new player! Arlo's suiting up to play!"

Mr. Butterworth stopped dead on his skates. He did this by crashing into the boards. "Arlo? You mean, Arlo's coming out to play?"

All the kids on the ice stopped too. "Arlo? You're kidding! He's actually going to play?" No one could believe it. And I didn't want to believe it.

Cassie nearly flew across the ice and stopped by the rink's gate. "Arlo! You're actually going to play! I knew you would! Some kids said you didn't have the guts, but now you can show them!"

My brain kept whirling around and around and around, trying to figure out an escape. But no matter how hard I tried, I couldn't think of a way out. It was unavoidable. I, Arlo Billingsly, would be going out on the ice and making a complete fool of myself! My nightmare was coming to life!

I thought about faking a heart attack, but I knew that wouldn't work. Mrs. Armstrong was on to me. She could tell, just like Mom, when I was making stuff up.

As I looked around the schoolyard, hoping to come up with an idea to get out of this jam, I glanced at the Dumpster. The lid was open a crack. X would be watching everything I did. Not only was I going to make a fool of myself playing hockey, but I would be failing my third test. Everyone was looking at me, waiting while I laced up my skates. I couldn't exactly say, "Hold it! I'll be back in five minutes, right after I've climbed up on the gym roof and thrown a dozen raw eggs at all of you!" I didn't think that would work.

My last chance at becoming a Dumpster Dude was slipping away. X would never give me another one. Tomorrow at recess, I wouldn't be welcome in the Dumpster. I'd be a failed Dumpster Dude and a joke of a hockey player. I'd be an outcast. I'd be one of those kids everyone avoids. I'd be one of those kids who gets picked on and nobody cares. I'd be the type of kid everyone thinks is weird.

"Come on, Arlo! Hurry up!" Cassie yelled. For a second, I thought of stalling. Maybe if I took a really long time to lace up my skates, spring would arrive and the ice would melt. But Mrs. Armstrong foiled that plan by grabbing my boots, yanking them off and jamming my feet into the skates. She reefed on the laces so hard I thought my ankles would be crushed to a pulp. "The laces have got to be tight," she said. "You want good ankle support."

Next she grabbed both my wrists and pulled me off the bench and up onto my feet.

Amazing! I was actually standing up on a pair of skates! And the skates felt pretty good. A little clunky, but not bad. Mrs. Armstrong handed me my gloves and stick. Then she stuck a helmet on my head and did up the chin strap. "You're all set, Arlo. And don't forget hockey's number one rule."

"What's that?" I asked, hoping she'd tell me something that would instantly transform me into a real hockey player.

"Have fun!"

"Yeah. Sure," I mumbled nervously.

As I shuffled across sheets of plywood toward the ice, kids started to hoot, whistle, cheer and bang their sticks on the ice. "Yeah, Arlo! Way to go!" Cassie's voice rose above all the others. I felt like a complete klutz, clunking along the walkway. The skates were pretty awkward to walk on, and I was still on solid ground. What would it be like on the slippery ice?

Mrs. Armstrong swung the gate open as I reached the boards. I looked out across the glistening sheet of ice; it seemed like one great big banana peel stretching out forever. Tucking my stick under one arm, I groped with both hands to hold on to the edge of the boards. I stepped out with my right foot, very gingerly placing it on the ice.

"It's okay, Arlo!" Mr. Butterworth called. "You won't fall through the ice!"

Very slowly—and I mean VERY slowly—I lifted my left foot off the plywood and onto the ice.

I'd done it! I was actually standing on the ice in skates! Another cheer went up from the adults and some of the kids. The most amazing thing was that after ten seconds, I was still standing!

"Move your feet, Arlo," Mr. Butterworth called. "You can't spend the whole game standing in one spot."

I loosened my grip on the boards and took my stick in both hands. Resting the blade of my stick on the ice, I found I could lean on the stick, which gave me a little better balance. Carefully, I moved my right foot forward a few inches, then my left, then my right again, then my left. I was actually moving across the ice! And I was going forward! I wouldn't exactly call it skating. It was more like a shuffle. But I figure you have to start somewhere.

"There he goes! Arlo's on the move!" Mrs. Armstrong shouted.

When I was a few feet from the safety of the boards, I stopped shuffling my feet and a strange thing happened. The skates kept moving. They were actually gliding on the ice. Hey! Now I really was skating!

"Way to go, Arlo! That's the spirit!" Mr. Butterworth called.

"Yo! Arlo!" another kid called out. A few more hooted encouragement. I couldn't tell who they were because my eyes were fixed on the toes of my skates and the few inches of ice ahead. If I looked up, I knew I'd go crashing to the ice.

"We get Arlo on our team!" Cassie yelled. I could tell her voice anywhere because it sounded like the combination of a police siren and a chain saw. "We're going that way!" she yelled, but I couldn't look up to see which way she was pointing.

Mr. Butterworth dropped the puck and the game began. Kids were zooming past me like I was a statue.

"Arlo!" someone called. "The puck!"

I glanced up and saw the small rubber disk sliding across the ice toward me. Here was my first big chance to hit the puck! I figured, Why not go big for my first time out? So I drew my stick back, winding up for a slap shot. As soon as I lifted my stick off the ice, my feet suddenly slipped out from under me. As I went crashing to the ice, I took a wild swing at the puck. *Whoosh*! All I hit was air. Although my stick completely missed, I felt the puck bounce off my skate and slither over to Cassie.

"Nice pass, Arlo!" she called, racing off down the ice with the puck on her stick.

I felt a hand grab my arm and yank me to my feet. It was Mr. Butterworth. "Don't worry, Arlo. You'll get the hang of it!" he said, skating off.

I glanced up from my skates and saw that I was facing the wrong way. Taking baby steps, I slowly turned myself to face the other direction. Still leaning on my stick,

I pushed with my skates. Away I went, gliding along. And I was even going fast enough to feel a bit of wind on my face.

"Arlo!" A kid named Scott passed the puck ahead to me. I lifted my stick again and took another wild swing.

Whack! It was the sound of wood hitting rubber. I had actually hit the puck with my stick! Now this was a real accomplishment.

"Oh yeah!" I could hear some of the kids cheer. I didn't see where the puck went. On the follow-through, my skates slipped out from under me again, and I hit the ice like a belly-flopping elephant.

Somehow the puck ended up on Darren's stick, right in front of the net. He did a quick backhand, sliding the puck between the goalie's legs and into the back of the net.

"Nice pass, Arlo!" he shouted, pumping his fist in the air.

"An assist!" Cassie screamed. "Arlo's first assist!"

I couldn't believe it. I'd only been in the game for about three minutes, and already I had my first assist! I wondered if this was how Wayne Gretzky got his start. Probably not.

My next problem was learning how to get up off my stomach and back onto my feet. Mr. Butterworth was busy tying another kid's skate lace, so I was on my own this time. I discovered getting up on ice was a lot different than getting up on dry land. Every time I got my feet under me, I'd slowly push up with my hands.

Sometimes my hands would slip away and I'd go face first down to the ice. Other times I'd be just about up on my feet when...*whoosh*!...my skates took off and I'd be flat on the ice again. After my fourth attempt at standing up, Chuck came and stopped right by my head, spraying me with a shower of snow. "You look more like a beached whale than a hockey player!" he laughed as he skated off. I must have been up and down at least ten more times before some helping hand grabbed my arm and gave me a boost.

"Thanks!" I said. I never knew who it was. They were gone before I could turn around.

I took a few more steps. Hey! This skating was getting easier by the minute! I figured I'd be skating like the pros by the end of PE class. A few more strides, and I was actually picking up speed! Faster and faster I went across the ice. This was great!

I looked up and saw I was headed at top speed right for the goal. This wouldn't have been a problem except for two skills I hadn't learned yet—turning and stopping.

Elsa was playing goal, and I slammed into her, body-checking her right into the back of the net. "I do a pretty good imitation of a puck, don't I?" I said, but Elsa didn't laugh.

I guess she'd forgotten all about Mrs. Armstrong's number one rule.

It took a few minutes for Elsa and me to get untangled and out of the net. Once I was back on the ice, I set off again.

The more I skated, the better I felt. I could even dig the edges of my blades into the ice and swerve a little. I pushed harder on my right foot. The harder I pushed on my right foot, the more I turned to the left.

"Arlo!" someone shouted. I looked up and saw the puck sliding slowly toward me. My stick was in perfect position as the puck stopped right on the blade.

"Try to stickhandle!" Cassie shouted. Mr. Butterworth ordered everyone to back away, so there I was in a clearing on the ice. Here was my chance to make a big play. Stickhandle through the entire team and score a spectacular goal! I'd seen hockey on TV. I knew how it was done!

Pushing my left foot, I started to glide. And as I glided along, I pushed the puck with my stick. This was great! It would be an end-to-end rush, stickhandling through their entire team!

I skated down the ice, showing some smooth stickhandling, just like my favorite Canuck...OOPS! One problem. I'd forgotten the puck.

I was so worried about what my skates were doing, I'd left the puck behind at center ice. No problem! I would make a sharp right turn. And then I remembered another important fact. I could only turn left. My body turned right, but my skates kept on going straight. I looked like a penguin trying to fly, hitting the ice flat on my stomach and sliding along. Yes! Just as I feared! I had become a human Zamboni!

But still, no one laughed! No one teased. Not even Chuck or Elsa. No one called me a klutzomaniac, goof, bonehead, goonball or any other name. I was both right and wrong about these kids. They really were weird—but in a good way.

As the game went on, my skating slowly got better. I could turn left really well, and I even managed to stop once without slamming into the boards. I was also way better at getting up off the ice. That's because I had a lot of practice.

"Three more minutes!" Mr. Butterworth shouted.

With time running out, I skated toward the other team's goal. Lisa had the puck in the corner and passed it to me in front of the goal. I watched the puck slide in my direction, but just before it arrived, both my feet shot out from under me. Down to the ice I went with a *THUNK*! As I lay flat on my back, I took a blind swing with my stick.

Thwhack!

Yes! I had connected! The puck flippy-flopped toward the goal like an injured duck. Elsa went for the fluttering puck, but it somehow squirted between her pads. I could see it. It was behind her! The puck was sliding toward the goal line! By the time Elsa turned around, the puck had stopped dead, sitting motionless on the ice.

Everyone on my team erupted into screams, yells and whistles as we looked at that puck sitting two inches over the goal line. I had actually scored a goal! Who cares if it looked more like a curling shot than a hockey shot? It had gone over the goal line, and that's what mattered! A goal was a goal no matter how you scored it!

The team mobbed me with slaps on the back and high fives. This was great! Of course, Chuck had to skate past and spray me with snow again. "It was just beginner's luck," he said. "Plus, Elsa's the worst goalie in the known universe." But he was grinning as he said it.

I just smiled back at Chuck. I didn't care what he said because I had just made a great discovery. Hockey was fun! It was even better than eating peanut butter and banana sandwiches! It was even better than smushing a cream pie in someone's face! It was even better than throwing eggs off the roof of the gym.

And then, I remembered...

CHAPTER 16

S lowly, carefully, I put a hand in one of my pockets. Slimy ooze and bits of shell. Raw scrambled eggs. It was the same story for the rest of my pockets. One dozen raw scrambled eggs. The smashed eggs had soaked through, leaving damp patches on the outside of my jacket.

But the smashed eggs didn't worry me half as much as the thought of X spying on me. He had probably seen and heard everything: my first steps on the ice, my first pass, my first assist, my first goal. He would know I had not gone up on the gym roof and chucked eggs at the hockey game. He would know I had played hockey. But the worst part was he would know I was having fun.

I knew X would be really mad at me. I wasn't so sure about Rocko and Pinball. If they saw me flipping and flopping all over the ice and still having fun, maybe hanging out in the Dumpster with X wouldn't seem so great. Maybe they'd be willing to give hockey another chance.

I hated to think of what X would do to me. Knowing how he operated, he'd probably make my life at school miserable. Wherever I went, whatever I did, X would be watching. And eventually he'd come after me when I wasn't looking, just when I least expected it.

To make the situation even worse, I still didn't know who X was. At least if I knew his name or recognized his face, I could look out for him. But for now, X's identity was still an unsolved mystery.

As we left the ice and walked across the plywood to the benches to untie our skates, it was tough to tell exactly how I felt. On the one hand, I couldn't help but glance toward the Dumpster and think about Rocko, Pinball and X and how much I wanted to belong somewhere—even if it was a Dumpster. On the other hand, it actually felt like I could belong in this school. I was afraid, relieved, happy and uncertain all at the same time. I think you call that "mixed emotions."

"That was a very gutsy effort, Arlo," Mr. Butterworth said. "You should be very proud of yourself."

Mrs. Armstrong's smile was wider than I'd ever seen it before. "Arlo! You were wonderful! I can tell you're one of those natural athletes. But why do you have all those strange wet patches on your jacket?"

"Ah, it must be sweat. I sweat a lot," I said. Mrs. Armstrong smiled, looking like she actually believed me.

Cassie stood up on a bench and yelled, "And now, ladies and gentlemen! The three stars of today's game!

The third star...Mr. Butterworth!"

Everyone cheered.

"The second star...ME!"

Everyone booed.

"And the first star...rookie of the year, Arlo Billingsly!"

The cheering was louder than ever.

"Okay, everyone! Time to get back to class!" Mrs. Armstrong announced.

We sat down to take off our skates, and everyone was yapping about the game.

"Remember when I hit the post on that breakaway? I had the goalie beat!"

"I couldn't believe that pass Alan put right on my stick from center ice!"

"Did you see the glove save Ann made on Penelope? Too bad there weren't any NHL scouts here today or they would have offered her a contract on the spot!"

"Yeah!" I said. "And did you see the pass Alice gave me from the corner? Tape to tape! Too bad I was flat on my back on the ice!" Everyone laughed, but they weren't laughing *at* me. They were actually laughing *with* me.

"And a warning to all goaltenders!" Elsa shouted. "If you see Arlo headed for the net, GET OUT OF HIS WAY!"

We laughed so hard, we almost split our guts. There were enough stories to keep us talking about the game for at least a week. But I couldn't help glancing over at that Dumpster and wondering what the mysterious X was planning for me next. And what did Rocko and Pinball think of my performance on the ice?

"Move along, everyone!" Mr. Butterworth called. "Get your skates off and head back into the classroom as quickly as possible. The garbage truck's coming through."

As I tugged at the laces of my skates, trying to undo the jumbled knot Mrs. Armstrong had tied, I heard a roar and a rumble. A huge garbage truck was pulling into the schoolyard, slowly edging its way toward the Dumpster. Two forks stuck out from the front of the truck and slid underneath the Dumpster. Very slowly, the powerful metal forks lifted the Dumpster, ready to tilt it over and empty it into the back of the garbage truck. The next stop would be the compressor.

"STOP!" I shouted.

Everyone froze and looked at me—everyone except the driver of the garbage truck, that is. He just kept controlling the huge forks, lifting the Dumpster higher and higher. I jumped up from the bench and cupped my hands around my mouth.

"STOP! Don't dump that Dumpster!" I screamed. But ever so slowly, the Dumpster was being lifted higher and higher into the air. I'd seen it before: The Dumpster goes up and over the cab of the truck. The lid flips open, and everything inside the Dumpster falls into the back of the truck. X, Rocko and Pinball might have done some pretty wild stunts at the school, but I didn't think they'd be too crazy about being dropped from the Dumpster and buried in garbage in the back of this truck.

I grabbed my hockey stick and ran toward the truck. When I fell flat on my face, I remembered I was still wearing my skates. Back on my feet in a flash, I was clomping across the parking lot toward the truck.

"Arlo! Stop! You're ruining your skate blades!" Mrs. Armstrong called. I didn't have time to explain. I kept yelling and waving my stick, shuffling across that parking lot as fast as my skate blades could carry me. I was doing everything I could to get the attention of the truck driver, but he just stared at that Dumpster as it was lifted higher and higher.

By now the Dumpster was way off the ground and beginning to tip. There wouldn't be time for me to run the rest of the way to the truck before it was too late for X, Rocko and Pinball. There was only one thing I could do. I held my brand-new hockey stick like a spear, reared back and chucked it at the Dumpster with everything I had. My stick sailed gracefully through the air until it banged into the side of the Dumpster with a loud BOOM! Immediately the great forks lifting the Dumpster stopped moving. The Dumpster just hung there, suspended in midair.

The driver rolled down his window and shouted, "Hey, kid! What the heck do you think you're doing?"

"Just lower the Dumpster back down and I can explain!" I called back.

"Arlo! I hope you've got a very good explanation for this!" Mr. Butterworth said. He stood on one side of me, while Mrs. Armstrong stood on the other.

"Yes, Arlo. You'd better have a very good reason for…" Mrs. Armstrong didn't finish her sentence. Just before the Dumpster touched back down on the ground, the lid popped open, and out tumbled Pinball and Rocko.

"Waldo! Byron! What in the world…!" Mr. Butterworth shouted. Mrs. Armstrong didn't say anything. Her mouth just hung open in shock.

I kept my eyes on that Dumpster, for I knew there would be a third person climbing out—the mysterious X. This would be my chance to finally see what X looked like in broad daylight.

Pinball and Rocko got up off the ground, rubbing their heads after their clumsy escape from the clutches of the Dumpster. I'm an expert on clumsy, and their tumble out of the Dumpster onto the parking lot definitely qualified them for klutzhood.

Mr. Butterworth, Mrs. Armstrong and I all ran to Pinball and Rocko. Mrs. Armstrong got there first because she was the only one not wearing skates. Pinball's and Rocko's eyes were bugging out—I mean, they had a look of terror in their eyes I hadn't seen since the day my mom found a live snake in the kitchen cupboard of our old apartment. I figured Rocko and Pinball were terrified for a bunch of reasons. Maybe they were still scared from their close call with the garbage truck. Or maybe it was the sight of a very angry Mrs. Armstrong closing in on them. Or maybe they were afraid of what X would do to them later. Maybe it was all those things. Whatever the reasons, Rocko and Pinball looked like they were ready to make a run for it.

"Waldo and Byron!" Mrs. Armstrong shouted. "What in the name of..."

I was beginning to wonder if X really was in the Dumpster. Maybe he'd escaped before the garbage truck arrived. Maybe he had known the truck was coming at a different time this week.

But then I saw the lid of the Dumpster slowly open a crack. Then it opened further. I could see an arm pushing the lid up. Finally, up and over the edge of the Dumpster and down onto the ground fell the person I had known as X.

"Why, Cedric! What are you doing in there?" Mrs. Armstrong said. "I thought you were at a doctor's appointment."

Mrs. Armstrong was certainly shocked at seeing Cedric tumble out of that Dumpster, but not half as shocked as I was.

"Cedric?" I said. "You're X?"

He slowly got to his feet and, like Rocko and Pinball, stood with his hands behind his back, his eyes staring down at the tops of his boots.

I hadn't known Mr. Butterworth and Mrs. Armstrong for very long, but I was truly surprised that two such pleasant, friendly, cheerful people could look so angry. It was downright scary.

Even through his snowpants, I could tell Rocko's knees were shaking like crazy. Pinball's lower lip was trembling, and a great big tear trickled down Cedric's cheek.

"You boys have a lot of explaining to do," Mr. Butterworth said. "What you've done is a very serious..."

Then I did something I know I'm never supposed to do. I interrupted my principal.

"Did you guys find the book?" I said. Cedric, Waldo and Byron all looked at me like I was more than a little crazy.

I turned to Mr. Butterworth and said, "I signed a book out of the library yesterday and put it in my lunch bag. After I'd eaten my lunch, I threw the bag in the garbage. When Cedric, Waldo and Byron heard about my lost book, they told me not to worry. They'd find it for me."

Mr. Butterworth and Mrs. Armstrong were looking what you'd call skeptical—I could tell they didn't completely believe me. I'd seen that look on my mom's face about a million times. My story obviously needed more work.

"These guys knew how hard it was for me to come to a new school and not exactly fit in. So they decided to make me feel more welcome by helping me out. That's why they were searching through the Dumpster for my lost library book."

After another close examination of Mr. Butterworth's

and Mrs. Armstrong's faces, I thought they just might be softening up a little.

"Although it sounds extremely far-fetched, Arlo," Mr. Butterworth said, "if these boys have made you feel more welcome at the school, that's wonderful."

I could see a look of relief come over the Dumpster Dudes' faces.

"As for rummaging through the Dumpster, that is certainly something we don't allow at this school," Mr. Butterworth continued. "May I suggest welcoming Arlo to our school by engaging in safer activities that do not break any school rules." Mr. Butterworth wasn't smiling when he said this. I had a funny feeling he knew more than he was letting on.

"Yeah. Instead of rummaging around in the Dumpster," I said, "why don't you guys come out and play some hockey? I can demonstrate how you, too, can become the next human Zamboni!"

When Mom picked me up at the end of the day, she said, "Arlo? What happened to your jacket?"

I didn't make up any excuses. I didn't try to lie my way out of it. Instead I said, "If you don't mind, Mom, a bunch of us want to stay behind and play some hockey on the school rink for a while."

Mom's jaw dropped, and her mouth became a great big cavern of disbelief.

"Do you remember Nate? The kid who asked me over to his party? He lives a couple of houses down from us, so we'll walk home together afterward."

Mom was still speechless.

"And then, maybe you and I can go out to Bubba's Drive-in for supper. I hear he makes this amazing burger called Bubba's Blubber Burger. Don't worry. It's not made with whale meat. It's about as big as a whale, though."

Mom's face slowly lost its look of shocked amazement, and she broke into a smile bright enough to light up the highway all the way back to Victoria. It was more than just a smile of happiness. It was a smile of relief. I'd finally taken the first slippery step to making East Bend my new home.

EPILOGUE

A couple of months later, I got my first report card from East Bend Elementary School. My grades weren't any better than before, and I still couldn't do double-digit multiplication. But Mom said it was the best report card I'd ever gotten, all because of the comments Mrs. Armstrong had written:

Arlo has been a wonderful addition to our class. He is a very caring and generous boy. Our custodian, Mr. Ludlow, and our librarian, Ms. Springer, have appreciated the help Arlo has given them before and after school. It is wonderful to see a child act out of the goodness of his heart.

Arlo should be congratulated for working along with Byron, Waldo and Cedric to win second prize in the regional science fair for their project "Forget the Dumpster: Reducing Garbage in Schools Through Recycling."

It has also been wonderful to watch Arlo take part in our hockey games. He has shown great improvement since his first game, and next year I'm sure Arlo will be able to turn not only to the left, but also to the right.

I told Mom not to worry. Although I couldn't make any promises about the double-digit multiplication, I could almost guarantee her that by the end of next season, I'd be able to turn both ways.

Chris McMahen is an elementary school teacher-librarian living near Armstrong, British Columbia. When he's not busy writing, teaching or spending time with his family, he can be found cycling the back roads of the Spallumcheen Valley or making peculiar pottery. *Klutzhood* is his second novel for children.